Long ago and ...

the story goes, th... and laughter and ... land and hiding it ... adapted to their ... —and they thrived. They stayed hidden, but sometimes outsiders spotted them, leading to the legends of the sea.

Yet though the people were peaceful, trouble came about. Should they contact the outer lands? When the last battle began, the king of this land—of Pacifica—sent his four children far away in order to protect them. He didn't send them alone—they had guardians and talismans for protection.

But the world was harsher than King Okeana expected, and his children were left bereft. The two youngest daughters didn't remember their homeland, and the oldest daughter and son had memories of anger and loss and pain.

Now, however, it was time for the siblings to be reunited—to come home to reclaim what was lost...if they dared!

A Tale of the Sea

MORE THAN MEETS THE EYE by *Carla Cassidy*
IN DEEP WATERS by *Melissa McClone*
CAUGHT BY SURPRISE by *Sandra Paul*
FOR THE TAKING by *Lilian Darcy*

Dear Reader,

We have some incredibly fun and romantic Silhouette Romance titles for you this July. But as excited as we are about them, we also want to hear from ***you!*** Drop us a note—or visit www.eHarlequin.com—and tell us which stories you enjoyed the most, and what you'd like to see from us in the future.

We know you love emotion-packed romances, so don't miss Cara Colter's CROWN AND GLORY cross-line series installment, *Her Royal Husband*. Jordan Ashbury had no idea the man who'd fathered her child was a prince—until she reported for duty at his palace! Carla Cassidy spins an enchanting yarn in *More Than Meets the Eye*, the first of our A TALE OF THE SEA, the must-read Silhouette Romance miniseries about four very special siblings.

The temperature's rising not just outdoors, but also in Susan Meier's *Married in the Morning*. If the ring on her finger and the Vegas hotel room were any clue, Gina Martin was now the wife of Gerrick Green! Then jump into Lilian Darcy's tender *Pregnant and Protected,* about a fiery heiress who falls for her bodyguard....

Rounding out the month, Gail Martin crafts a fun, lighthearted tale about two former high school enemies in *Let's Pretend....* And we're especially delighted to welcome new author Betsy Eliot's *The Brain & the Beauty*, about a young mother who braves a grumpy recluse in his dark tower.

Happy reading—and please keep in touch!

Mary-Theresa Hussey

Mary-Theresa Hussey
Senior Editor

Please address questions and book requests to:
Silhouette Reader Service
U.S.: 3010 Walden Ave., P.O. Box 1325, Buffalo, NY 14269
Canadian: P.O. Box 609, Fort Erie, Ont. L2A 5X3

More Than Meets the Eye

CARLA CASSIDY

Published by Silhouette Books
America's Publisher of Contemporary Romance

Special thanks and acknowledgment are given to Carla Cassidy for her contribution to the A TALE OF THE SEA series.

To Carlee,
The newest light in my life.
Thank you for being a grandchild whom I can love and spoil and adore—then send home. I love you!

SILHOUETTE BOOKS

ISBN 0-373-19602-4

MORE THAN MEETS THE EYE

This edition published by arrangement with Harlequin Books S.A.

Visit Silhouette at www.eHarlequin.com

Printed in U.S.A.

Books by Carla Cassidy

Silhouette Romance

Patchwork Family #818
Whatever Alex Wants... #856
Fire and Spice #884
Homespun Hearts #905
Golden Girl #924
Something New #942
Pixie Dust #958
The Littlest Matchmaker #978
The Marriage Scheme #996
Anything for Danny #1048
**Deputy Daddy* #1141
**Mom in the Making* #1147
**An Impromptu Proposal* #1152
**Daddy on the Run* #1158
Pregnant with His Child... #1259
Will You Give My Mommy a Baby? #1315
‡*Wife for a Week* #1400
The Princess's White Knight #1415
Waiting for the Wedding #1426
Just One Kiss #1496
Lost in His Arms #1514
An Officer and a Princess #1522
More Than Meets the Eye #1602

Silhouette Shadows

Swamp Secrets #4
Heart of the Beast #11
Silent Screams #25
Mystery Child #61

*The Baker Brood
‡Mustang, Montana
†Sisters
**The Delaney Heirs

Silhouette Intimate Moments

One of the Good Guys #531
Try To Remember #560
Fugitive Father #604
Behind Closed Doors #778
†*Reluctant Wife* #850
†*Reluctant Dad* #856
‡*Her Counterfeit Husband* #885
‡*Code Name: Cowboy* #902
‡*Rodeo Dad* #934
In a Heartbeat #1005
‡*Imminent Danger* #1018
Strangers When We Married #1046
****Man on a Mission* #1077
Born of Passion #1094
***Once Forbidden* #1115
***To Wed and Protect* #1126
***Out of Exile* #1149

Silhouette Desire

A Fleeting Moment #784
Under the Boardwalk #882

Silhouette Books

Shadows 1993
"Devil and the Deep Blue Sea"

The Loop

Getting it Right: Jessica

Silhouette Yours Truly

Pop Goes the Question

The Coltons

Pregnant in Prosperino

CARLA CASSIDY

is an award-winning author who has written over thirty-five books for Silhouette. In 1995, she won Best Silhouette Romance from *Romantic Times* for *Anything for Danny*. In 1998, she also won a Career Achievement Award for Best Innovative Series from *Romantic Times*.

Carla believes the only thing better than curling up with a good book to read is sitting down at the computer with a good story to write. She's looking forward to writing many more books and bringing hours of pleasure to readers.

A TALE OF THE SEA

Family Tree

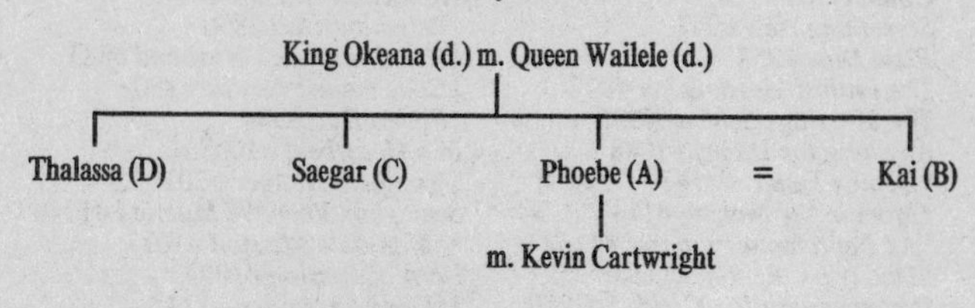

(A) More Than Meets the Eye
SR #1602, On sale 7/02

(B) In Deep Waters
SR #1608, On sale 8/02

(C) Caught by Surprise
SR #1614, On sale 9/02

(D) For the Taking
SR #1620, On sale 10/02

KEY:
m. Married
d. Deceased
= Twins

KINGDOM OF PACIFICA
135°
N
Hawaiian Islands
NORTH AMERICA
PACIFIC OCEAN
PACIFICA
0° Equator
SOUTH AMERICA
French Polynesian Islands
All underlined places are fictitious.

Chapter One

A wild-goose chase.

Kevin Cartwright feared that's exactly what he was indulging in when he entered the automatic doors of the Kansas City Memorial Hospital.

After three years of false leads and dashed hopes, he really didn't expect this new development to pan out. But the moment he'd seen her on television, he'd known he had to check her out.

"I'm here for an appointment with Dr. Phoebe Jones," he said to the lobby receptionist.

"Her office is on the fourth floor," the elderly woman explained. "Take the elevator up then ask at the nurses' station and they'll direct you to Dr. Jones's office."

A moment later Kevin stood in the elevator and

stifled a yawn with the back of his hand. It was only noon, but he'd already been on a plane for five hours. Apparently the good doctor only took appointments during her lunch hour and so he'd had to take a red-eye flight to get from Southern California to Kansas City before noon.

He tried to ignore the antiseptic smell that permeated the building, the "hospital" scent evoking in him memories of intense pain and crippling fear.

Don't think about it, he told himself. Just don't think about it. There was no way he wanted to fall back into memories of that time so long ago.

He found the nurses' station on the fourth floor with no problem and was taken to Dr. Jones's office by one of the nurses.

The office was small, furnished simply with a desk, two chairs, and a wall of bookcases behind the desk. The bookcases held nothing but medical tombs, the desk, a computer, and an appointment book.

There were no personal artifacts, no photos, no vase of flowers...nothing to indicate anything about the woman who belonged to the office.

Even in here, the hospital smell lingered and Kevin felt the unwelcome memories once again trying to intrude. It had been five years ago that he'd last been in a hospital and it vaguely surprised him that the memories were so strong that it felt as if it had only been yesterday.

He consciously shoved them away and focused on

the task at hand. She's got to be the right one, he thought as he sat in the chair opposite the desk.

Adrenaline pumped through him as he anticipated that after three long years, it was possible he'd finally found one of the four people he'd been hired to find.

"Good afternoon." The soft, feminine voice drifted from the doorway and a second later she stepped into his sight.

"Hello," he returned, half rising from his seat. His pulse accelerated slightly as he gazed at her.

He told himself it had nothing to do with the fact that she was one sexy-looking woman, but rather because it was possible he was finally going to be successful in partially wrapping up one of his most difficult cases.

Still, she was certainly easy on the eyes.

She waved him back down as she eased into the chair behind her desk. "I'm Dr. Jones and you must be Kevin Cartwright."

"Yes, that's right." He couldn't see the necklace. Beneath the smock she wore, she had on a green turtleneck that did dazzling things to her green eyes, but hid the necklace that had brought him to her in the first place.

"What can I do for you, Mr. Cartwright?" She opened up an appointment book and stared down. "According to my secretary, you were quite insistent on meeting me today, but you were vague about the purpose for this meeting."

She tucked a strand of honey-colored hair behind her ear, then looked at him once again. In her eyes he saw a no-nonsense directness. ''If you're from a drug company, I can tell you right now that I don't do the ordering and so we'd be wasting each other's time.''

''No, I'm not from any company. I saw the news story about the little boy who lost his arm in a mowing accident. You and your team of doctors made national news with the successful surgery to reattach the limb.''

She nodded. ''Michael is a good kid and we were very happy with the success of the operation.''

''It sounds as if Michael is a little fighter.'' For the first time since he'd walked into the office, she smiled and Kevin felt the force of that gorgeous smile in the pit of his stomach.

''He certainly is,'' she agreed.

''The television screen didn't do you justice.'' He hadn't meant to say it, but it was what had been going around in his head.

She was thinner than she'd looked on television, although she certainly had curves in all the right places. And there was no way the television screen had been able to capture the intense green of her eyes or the soft golden glow of her shoulder-length hair.

The smile that had momentarily lifted the corners of her lush lips disappeared abruptly at his words. ''What is it you want, Mr. Cartwright?'' She glanced at the delicate silver watch on her wrist. ''I have another surgery scheduled in exactly fifteen minutes.''

''I think you're the woman I've been looking for,'' he explained.

The coolness on her pretty features intensified. ''Is that some sort of a pick-up line?'' She grasped the phone and he knew he was mere seconds from being escorted out of the place by security.

''No! Of course not,'' he protested, realizing how it sounded to her. First he tells her the television screen didn't do her justice, then he tells her she's the girl he's been looking for...she probably thought he was some sort of crazed stalker. ''What I meant to say is that I think you are one of the people I've been trying to find for the past three years. I'm a private investigator, Dr. Jones, and three years ago a man contacted me and hired me to find four siblings.''

''Siblings?'' For the first time her eyes lit with interest.

He nodded. ''Three sisters and a brother.''

She sat back in her chair and gazed at him intently. ''And you think it's possible that I might be one of those siblings?''

''Yes, I think it's possible. I know the woman I'm looking for has the first name of Phoebe.'' But, he'd also been told that the people he sought would probably live near the ocean, and Kansas City, Missouri, couldn't be farther away from an ocean.

A dainty frown appeared between her perfectly

arched pale eyebrows. ‘‘But, Phoebe isn’t such an odd name. There must be hundreds…thousands of women named Phoebe,’’ she protested, then looked at her watch once again. ‘‘And I really don’t have time to get into this right now.’’

She stood and he stood as well. He hadn’t been able to ask her about the necklace and that was the key to discovering if she was the Phoebe he was looking for.

‘‘Look, could we meet later this evening to discuss this further?’’ He could see the hesitation in her eyes. ‘‘We could meet some place public, and if you think I’m wasting your time, you’d be free to walk away.’’

She glanced at her watch once again, then looked back at him. ‘‘All right,’’ she agreed, although he could see the skepticism in her eyes. ‘‘There’s a little café called Myrtle’s not far from here. I’ll meet you there at seven.’’

‘‘What’s the address of this Myrtle’s?’’ he asked.

She smiled tightly. ‘‘You’re a private investigator, Mr. Cartwright, I’m sure you can manage to find it somehow.’’ With these words, she turned and disappeared out of the office.

Kevin stared after her, wondering just how difficult the doctor was going to be. As he left the office and stepped into the elevator, he reached into his pocket and withdrew a large chunk of gold nugget. The nugget had been his latest payment for his time and expenses.

He walked across the hospital lobby, then exited into the bright midday sunshine. He drew a deep breath of the early spring-scented air, grateful to leave the hospital and all its memory-stirring odors behind.

As he strode across the parking lot to his rental car, he worried the nugget between his fingers, his thoughts filled with the man who had given it to him.

Loucan. A strange name for a strange man. Initially when Kevin had been contacted by him and told that Loucan wanted to hire him to find four siblings, Kevin had thought nothing about it.

He'd been involved in finding people before—adopted children seeking their biological parents, parents wanting to find children. It was a large part of what he did as a private investigator.

But this case had been strange from the very beginning. Loucan had initially contacted him by phone and they had set up a meeting at a restaurant on the wharf in Santa Barbara.

The tall, powerfully built man had retained Kevin's services and had paid him with a handful of high-quality pearls. Since that time three years before, Kevin had met with Loucan several times a year and each time had been paid with perfect pearls, old gold coins, or gold nuggets.

Instantly, Kevin's ex-cop nose had smelled a mystery, but it was a mystery he had yet to crack. If Phoebe Jones had the necklace he'd thought he had spotted her wearing in the news report, then she was a piece of the puzzle.

He shoved the nugget back into his pocket, then got into his red rental car. At the moment, the biggest mystery he had to solve was to discover exactly where Myrtle's Café was located.

Phoebe stood beneath a hot shower spray in her bathroom, hoping the steamy water would wash away at least a little bit of her exhaustion.

Her morning had begun before five, when an emergency appendectomy had needed to be done. That had set the tone for the hectic day. Besides the three surgeries that had been planned well in advance, she'd had three more emergency surgeries to undergo.

Still, the exhaustion was nothing new. Working at an inner-city hospital, it was no secret that all the doctors and nurses were overworked and underpaid. The only thing that compensated for that was the incredible sense of satisfaction her work brought to her.

She stepped out of the shower and grabbed a fluffy blue towel. Drying off, she thought of the man who had been in her office at noon that day.

Kevin Cartwright. He was a devilishly handsome man, his light-brown hair a perfect foil for his deep blue eyes. In the first instant of seeing him sitting across from her desk, she'd felt an immediate magnetic pull toward him.

But now she wasn't sure if it had been the man

himself or the sweet possibility of his words that had drawn her to him.

Family. Was it possible she might have family members somewhere out there? She had given up hope of ever finding any a long time ago.

And now this good-looking stranger had appeared in her office and spoken a magic word...siblings. Sisters and a brother—it would be so wonderful.

She padded out of the bathroom and into the bedroom, where she had carefully laid out the clothes she was going to put on.

As she dressed, she steadfastly shoved thoughts of the possibility of finding family members aside, afraid to get her hopes up only to have them dashed once again.

It took her only a few minutes to pull on a pair of tan slacks and a green and tan flowered blouse. She ran a brush quickly through her shoulder-length blond hair, touched a dab of pink lipstick to her lips, then grabbed her purse and left her apartment.

Moments later she was out on the sidewalk headed toward Myrtle's. She'd moved into her apartment building when she'd been a resident at the hospital and money, or lack thereof, had been an issue.

The apartment building was not only walking distance to the hospital, but also to the café she frequented on a regular basis and a public library.

Even after her residency had ended and money woes had eased, she'd never considered moving from the small apartment building. She liked keeping things the way they were.

It was fifteen minutes before seven when she entered Myrtle's Café and took her usual seat by the window. From this vantage point she could see Kevin as he arrived.

"Hi, Dr. Jones," Camilla greeted her with a friendly smile as she poured Phoebe a glass of iced tea. "Long day?"

Phoebe smiled at the attractive older woman. "They're all long days."

"The usual?" Camilla asked.

"Yes, but could you wait to place the order? I'm meeting somebody."

One of Camilla's gray eyebrows danced upward. "Somebody of the male persuasion?"

"Yes, but it isn't what you think," Phoebe hurriedly said.

Camilla frowned in disappointment. "It's never what I think, and it's not right, a pretty young woman like you eating alone every night."

Phoebe smiled. "I don't mind. Most evenings I'm too tired to make good conversation with anyone."

"And I think you are selling yourself short, Dr. Jones," Camilla replied, then excused herself to hurry to another table.

Phoebe took a sip of her iced tea and gazed out the window. Camilla was constantly harping on her to get a life. What Camilla didn't understand was Phoebe had a life…a safe, comfortable life that revolved around her work.

There had been enough chaos in her life in the first eighteen years to last a lifetime.

Still, that didn't stop her pulse from accelerating slightly as she saw Kevin across the street. As she watched, he crossed the street, sauntering with a kind of loose-hipped gait she couldn't help but admire.

Although his legs were long and lean in his tight jeans, his upper body was muscular beneath the short-sleeved polo shirt. His bulging biceps peeked out just beneath the sleeves of the dark-blue cotton shirt.

As she watched, he paused just outside the front door of the café and quickly raked a hand through his light-brown hair, as if wanting to make certain he looked all right for his meeting with her.

Phoebe reached up and started to smooth her own hair, then jerked her hands back down as she realized what she was doing.

This meeting with Kevin Cartwright wasn't a date. She simply wanted any information he might be able to give her about the possibility of her having siblings.

He walked through the café front door, bringing with him an energy that seemed to electrify the entire establishment. She'd noticed that earlier about him…the energy that seemed to emanate from him.

He gazed around the café, then he found her and a smile curved the corners of his lips. He had a devastating smile. It transformed him from a handsome man into a sexy devil.

"I see you found it," she said as he slid into the chair opposite her at the small table.

"I'm not just a private investigator, I'm a good private investigator," he said and flashed her another of his seductive grins.

At that moment Camilla stopped at the table. "Evening," she said, then winked broadly at Phoebe, as if to indicate she approved of the way Kevin looked. "The specials this evening are meat loaf and barbecue chicken."

Kevin looked at Phoebe expectantly.

"I already ordered," she explained.

"She always gets the same thing," Camilla said.

"Then I'd just like a cheeseburger and fries," Kevin said as he handed Camilla back the menu. "And a cup of coffee to drink."

As Camilla hurried away, Kevin returned his attention to Phoebe, gazing at her without speaking for a long moment. She picked up her glass of iced tea and took a sip, her mouth unaccountably dry. She suddenly realized she was nervous.

She told herself it had nothing to do with Kevin, but rather with the information he might give her, information that might unite her with members of her family.

She set her glass back down and looked at him.

''All right, Mr. Cartwright, tell me again what brought you to me.''

''Please, make it Kevin,'' he replied. He leaned back in his chair and studied her. She felt her cheeks pinken beneath his obvious appraisal. ''You're very pretty,'' he finally said.

Her cheeks grew hotter. ''Do you always speak your mind so freely?''

His grin widened. ''Always, but I've made you uncomfortable and I apologize.''

She nodded stiffly, although she didn't think he sounded apologetic in the least. Suddenly he irritated her with his sexy smile and broad chest, with his flirting long-lashed eyes and five-o'clock shadow of whiskers.

''Mr. Cartwright, I'm a busy woman and I don't have time for nonsense. Now, you mentioned this afternoon that somebody had hired you to find a woman named Phoebe. What makes you think I'm the one you're searching for?''

He shrugged, his smile fading away. ''When I saw you on the news report, you looked to be around the right age of the woman I'm seeking.''

''I'm around twenty-seven.''

One of his eyebrows lifted. ''Around twenty-seven?''

Their conversation came to a halt as Camilla arrived at their table with their orders. She served

Phoebe's salad and soup first, then gave Kevin his cheeseburger, fries and coffee.

"You said you were around twenty-seven," he reminded her the moment Camilla had left them alone once again.

She nodded and broke apart the whole-wheat roll that had come with her salad. "I was raised in foster care and no birth certificate was ever found for me. Child protective services thought I was about two when I went into the system."

Kevin chewed a bite of cheeseburger and chased it with a sip of coffee. "How did you get into the system?" he asked.

"From what I was told, I was brought to a hospital severely ill. The woman who brought me in was also sick and later died. She was never identified." Phoebe stared down at her vegetable soup, fighting against the sadness that always threatened to overwhelm her when she thought of her past.

He leaned forward, so close that she could smell the scent of him, a spicy cologne tempered by spring sunshine and a hint of maleness. "So, you don't know if her name was Trealla?"

"Trealla..." The name rolled off her tongue, unfamiliar and yet somehow not totally alien. "I don't know...I really don't remember anything about my early childhood."

He popped a fry into his mouth and once again stared at her unabashedly. "There's one way for me to know if you're the woman I'm looking for,'' he said after a long moment of silence.

''And what's that?''

He reached into his shirt pocket and pulled out a folded sheet of paper. ''The woman I'm searching for has in her possession a piece of metal that looks like this.'' He unfolded the paper and shoved it over to her.

With trembling fingers, Phoebe picked up the paper and stared at the object drawn there. It was a fourth of a pie shape, with intricate designs that were as familiar to Phoebe as the sound of her own heartbeat.

Instantly her hand grabbed her chest, fingers fumbling for the charm that hung on the silver chain and nestled between her breasts.

She pulled the charm from its resting place and half rose, leaning across the table to show him. Her heart crashed frantically against her ribs. ''I'm the one you've been looking for, Kevin. You've found the right woman.''

Chapter Two

As Kevin compared the drawing on the paper to the actual piece of metal on the chain around her neck, a wave of excitement swept through him. The drawing on the paper perfectly matched the charm she wore.

He'd found her. After all his years of searching, after all the false leads and dashed hopes, he'd finally found one of the four he'd been hired to find.

In his exuberant high spirits, he reached across the small table and grabbed her hands in his. "We've got to get you to Southern California," he exclaimed.

"Whoa...wait." She pulled her hands from his, a touch of wariness...and something else in her sea-green eyes. She fumbled with her napkin in her lap, her eyes downcast. When she finally looked up at him again, her eyes sparkled overbrightly, as if she were on the verge of tears.

"I'm sorry," she said, her voice slightly husky. "You have to understand, I long ago gave up on ever finding any of my family. I thought I was all alone in the world. I—I'm a little bit afraid to get my hopes up."

In that instant Kevin had the ridiculous impulse to reach out and pull her to his chest, tell her that he would see to it that she was never alone in the world again.

He'd always been a sucker for vulnerable women.

However, a return visit to the hospital that afternoon had given him enough information to believe that Dr. Phoebe Jones was anything but vulnerable.

A loner, controlling, brusque, devoted, a rigid professional…those were just some of the terms her colleagues had used to describe her.

Still, there was no denying the well of emotions that now shone from her eyes, emotions that touched his heart. "You're smart not to get your hopes up yet," he said and speared a fry with his fork. "I've found you, but I haven't found the other three yet."

She shoved her barely eaten salad aside. "Tell me about the man who hired you. Is it possible he's my father?"

Her beautiful spring-colored eyes held his gaze intently and he wished he could tell her that it was a possibility, but he couldn't. "No, Loucan is far too young to be your father. He's about my age…around thirty-four or so."

"Loucan? Loucan what?"

"Just Loucan," Kevin replied, then frowned. One of the most frustrating things about this particular job was the fact that he hadn't been able to discover a thing about the man who had hired him. "Anyway, like I told you before, he hired me to find you and bring you to Santa Barbara."

Her face paled slightly. "I left California eleven years ago when I was sixteen and I swore I'd never go back."

"Loucan made it clear to me that he wanted you to come to him, and if not you, then I was to bring your necklace to him."

Her fingers clutched around the necklace. "I'm not about to give up the only thing I've had since my childhood to a man I haven't met. I don't know this Loucan, and I don't know you."

Kevin grinned. "I can't tell you much about Loucan, but I can tell you that I'm a good guy. I like children and animals and I only snore when sleeping on my back."

He was pleased to see a hint of a smile tug at her lips. "I certainly can't make a decision to take off for California based on whether you snore or not," she replied.

He leaned forward. "But, you have to admit that you're curious. I mean, maybe this Loucan is another brother, or a cousin. Can you really walk away from the opportunity to find out?"

He felt slightly guilty as he tried to decide if he wanted her to go to California to find her family, or if his sole reason for getting her there was the promise of an enormous payoff from Loucan.

"I don't know." She looked troubled. "I need some time to digest all this. I'm certainly not going to make a decision right now."

"Fair enough," he replied.

For the next few minutes they ate in silence. Despite the odors of cooking food that filled the café, Kevin could smell Phoebe's perfume, a soft, floral scent he found incredibly attractive.

In fact, he found everything about Dr. Phoebe Jones attractive, from the shiny strands of her blond hair, to her intensely green eyes. She ate with a precision he found fascinating, all her bites of salad carefully cut with a fork and a knife. She then pushed her salad away and began eating her soup.

"You mentioned you left California when you were sixteen," he said, breaking the silence that had grown to uncomfortable proportions between them.

She daintily dabbed her mouth with her napkin and nodded. "I graduated from high school when I was sixteen and petitioned the court for an order of emancipation. I had several scholarship offers for college and decided to come here and attend Kansas University, then transferred to KU med school and finished my residency at the hospital a little over a year ago."

"Quite an accomplishment for somebody so young," he observed.

She shrugged her slender shoulders. "I knew from the time I was young that I wanted to be a doctor. I just didn't let anything or anyone distract me from my ultimate goal."

"Any particular reason why you chose the medical field?" He wasn't sure why, but he suddenly wanted to know everything about her, what made her tick, what things she liked, what experiences had made her who she was.

"I was very sickly as a child. It seemed that my body didn't have the normal immunities to fight illness. All the childhood diseases hit me really hard and I spent much of my early years in hospitals for one reason or another."

She looked down at her salad, but not before he thought he saw a whisper of pain in her eyes. When she looked back at him, whatever he thought he'd seen was gone. "But enough about me," she said. "What about you? What made you decide to become a private investigator?"

"I heard it was a job that paid well for a small amount of work." It was his stock answer to anyone who asked him about his career choice. He never told anyone that it was a job he had taken when his life had been shattered and all his dreams had been destroyed.

"Are you from California?" she asked.

"Not originally. I was born and raised in Chicago and lived there until about five years ago when I moved to Los Angeles."

"What made you move?"

He grinned. "The promise of sun and surf and women in bikinis."

She eyed him intently. "Are you always so flippant?"

"Always. Life is too short to take anything too seriously."

"Life is too short not to take everything seriously," she countered.

She was gorgeous, and something about her filled him with a tension, but they obviously had nothing in common, he realized. All she was to him was a case that he wanted to see through to the end.

"Is there some way I can get in touch with you," she asked, breaking into his thoughts. "I really need some time to think about all this." She touched her lips with her napkin and placed the napkin next to her salad bowl.

"I'm staying at the Allis Plaza Hotel," he replied and motioned to the waitress. "But I'll walk you home."

"That's not necessary," she replied, again a touch of wariness in her eyes.

"Phoebe, if you're worried about me walking you home and discovering where you live, I already know where you live. Remember, I'm a private investigator."

"So, what else do you know about me?" she asked, but at that moment the waitress returned to their table.

Phoebe fought with him over the check, but relented and let him pay when he reminded her he had an expense account. Then, together they left the café and stepped out into the deepening shadows of falling night.

"You didn't answer my question," she reminded him as they walked leisurely along the deserted sidewalk. "What else have you managed to dig up about me besides my address?"

"You don't socialize with any co-workers. You're highly respected for your skills as a surgeon, but nobody seems to know much about you as a person. As far as your neighbors are concerned, you never have visitors in your home."

"You spoke with my neighbors?" she asked, a touch of outrage in her voice.

"It's what I do," he said without apology. "I use whatever means necessary to find out things about people. I speak to neighbors, go through garbage, stake out places. You were exceptionally easy to find out about because you are such a creature of habit."

"And that's bad?"

"That's terrible if somebody is going to plan to

perpetrate a crime against you. It makes you predictable."

"Well, I like my life just fine, thank you," she exclaimed with a touch of self-righteous anger. "And I would appreciate it if you didn't talk to any more of my neighbors or co-workers and if you kept your nose out of my garbage. If you want or need to know something about me or my life, ask me."

"It's a deal," he agreed easily as they came to her apartment building.

"Thank you for dinner," she said.

"No problem." He followed her through the door and into the lobby that held nothing but two elevators. He punched the up button on one of them, then smiled at her. "I'll see you up. I always see ladies to their front doors."

The elevator door opened and the two of them stepped inside. The scent that he'd noticed coming from her in the café was more pronounced in the small confines of the elevator and again Kevin felt an energy well up inside him.

This time he recognized it for what it was...an intense physical attraction. Although he didn't know her at all, made it a habit never to get involved with any of his cases, something about her made him think of tangled sheets and hot kisses.

"So, are you going to call this Loucan and tell him you found me?" she asked.

"Yeah, but I figured I'd wait to contact him until

you've decided what to do.'' The elevator doors whooshed open and together they stepped out into a narrow hallway.

They walked down the hall and stopped in front of apartment 505. She fumbled in her purse and pulled out her keys and quickly unlocked the door, then turned back to him. ''If I did agree to go to California, it would take a couple of days for me to arrange for somebody else to take care of my current patients and for me to clear my schedule.''

''Loucan has waited three years for me to find you. I'm sure he can wait a little while longer.'' He fought the impulse to reach out and touch the smooth skin of her cheek, stroke a silky strand of her hair.

Instead he shoved his hands in his pockets. ''Call me when you've made a decision,'' he said. ''Good night, Phoebe.''

''Good night, Kevin.''

He'd just turned to walk away when he heard her gasp. It wasn't the gasp of a woman happy to be home, but rather it was a gasp rife with surprise... with fear.

He whirled around and flew through her apartment door. Immediately he saw what had made her gasp. The place was wrecked and she didn't strike him as the kind of woman who would live in such utter chaos.

''You creep!'' Without warning she picked up a sofa cushion from the floor and flung it at him. ''Was this your plan? You meet me at Myrtle's and while you're buying my dinner your accomplice comes in here and robs me blind?'' Her eyes flashed with temper and her chest rose and fell rapidly.

''Don't be ridiculous,'' he snapped as he pulled his gun from his ankle holster. ''Call 911 and don't leave this room.'' He didn't wait for her to reply, but moved deeper into the apartment, wanting to make certain no perpetrator was still inside.

He checked the cabinets and pantry in the kitchen, the closet and shower in the bathroom, then moved into the bedroom.

The room was a vision in blues and peaches, but the dresser drawers had been emptied on the floor and a jewelry box on the top of the dresser had been upended.

Confirming that there was nobody in any of the rooms, he returned to the living room, where Phoebe stood in the middle of the mess looking shell-shocked.

''Did you call the police?'' he asked as he put his gun away.

She nodded. ''They should be here any minute.''

''Phoebe, I swear I had absolutely nothing to do with this,'' he said. He walked over to where she stood and placed his hands on her shoulders. He realized she was trembling. ''You must believe me,'' he said.

She stepped away from him and he dropped his

hands to his sides. She sighed, her gaze darting around the room. "I'm not sure why, but I do believe you."

Relief flooded through him. "While we wait for the police to arrive, you might want to look around and see if anything has been stolen. But try not to touch anything."

He watched as she walked around the room, a frown marring her forehead. By the time the police arrived, she had discerned that nothing had been taken.

Kevin wasn't surprised. His gut instinct told him this hadn't been a random burglary. Instead, it looked as if a frantic search had been conducted.

While Phoebe spoke with the officers, making out a report, Kevin's mind raced with possibilities. Was it merely a coincidence that he had found her today and her place had been searched this evening? Or, was it something more sinister? In finding Phoebe, had he also found her for somebody else?

It was after eleven when the police left and Phoebe shooed Kevin out the door. He'd offered several times to stay and help her straighten up the mess, but she'd declined. She needed time alone…time to assimilate the craziness of the day.

First there had been Kevin, with his amazing story of a man in California trying to find her, then the break-in. She felt as if she was in overdrive and what she needed more than anything was a good night's sleep.

But, there was no way she could give into sleep until her apartment was put back into some sort of order. Chaos made her nuts.

As she worked, she thought of everything that Kevin had told her. The thought that someplace out there she had a brother and sisters, pulled forth old emotions of want and need that she had spent years trying to repress.

As a child she'd been hungry for family, but by the time she'd reached twelve and with no family coming forth to claim her, she'd shoved away her hunger and focused instead on getting where she wanted to be, alone.

The idea of returning to California evoked in her an enormous dread. Her years spent there had not been happy ones.

But could she forget about a man named Loucan who might have knowledge about her mother and father, about any siblings she might have?

It was after one in the morning when she finally fell into bed, exhausted but comforted by the fact that her apartment was relatively back to normal.

Still, sleep remained elusive, her thoughts haunted by the knowledge that somebody had been in her private space, somebody had violated her home.

What had they wanted? If it had been a simple burglary why hadn't her television disappeared? Her stereo equipment or her computer? As far as she could tell, absolutely nothing had been stolen.

She fell asleep with questions nagging at her and awakened at six the next morning, gasping for air and covered with a light veil of perspiration.

The dream. It had been a while since she'd had the recurrent nightmare that had plagued her all her life. But, the moment consciousness claimed her, she knew she'd just suffered it again.

She didn't move from the bed for long moments, instead waited for the last vestiges of the dream to leave and her heartbeat to return to normal.

Eventually when she pulled herself from the tangle of sheets, she refused to dwell on the nightmare images and headed directly for the shower, hoping a cascade of hot water would effectively banish any lingering bad feeling the dream might have left behind.

Standing beneath the hot spray of water, her thoughts immediately turned to Kevin Cartwright. She wasn't sure what she thought about him. Granted, she found him very attractive, but she was certain they couldn't be less alike.

She was devoted to her work and he seemed rather irreverent about his. In fact, he'd seemed pretty irreverent about everything. Despite that, as crazy as it sounded, she trusted him.

And for just a moment when the police had left and the two of them had been standing in her living room, she'd desperately wished he would wrap his arms around her and pull her tight against his broad chest.

The wish had been nothing more than a crazy impulse brought on by the trauma of the home invasion. Definitely not likely to happen again, she thought moments later as she dressed in a pale-blue uniform.

She'd been taking care of herself since she'd been very young. As a foster child, she'd learned early on that she had nobody to depend on but herself. She learned to rock herself when she needed comforting, whisper to herself when she was lonely, and wrap her arms around herself when she desperately needed a hug. And the handsome Kevin Cartwright wasn't about to change old habits.

The sun was just peeking over the horizon as she left her apartment. She stepped out on the sidewalk and drew in a deep, cleansing breath.

She loved early mornings, when the air smelled crisp and clean and the streets were just starting to fill with people hurrying to work.

She took only a few steps, then halted as she spied Kevin getting out of a small red car parked at the curb. He looked rumpled and stiff and the slight five-o'clock shadow she'd noticed at dinner the night before had grown to full scruffy whiskered proportions.

What was he doing here? With the memory of her wanting him to hold her still fresh in her mind, his appearance irritated her. She eyed him coolly as he approached.

"Morning," he said, his voice slightly husky. He winced. "Is it always this bright in the mornings?"

"I gather you aren't normally an early riser," she replied dryly.

"Sure, I am. Early afternoon." He grinned and with his hair tousled and his growth of beard, and a sleepy cast to his eyes, Phoebe instantly knew what he would look like in bed. And the mental image that appeared in her head of him naked and between crisp white sheets was heart-stoppingly appealing and it only served to increase her irritation.

"You look like you slept in your car," she exclaimed.

He grinned, that half-crooked, devilish smile that set her on edge. "I did. It beats the price of a hotel room."

She scowled. "I told you, Kevin, that I needed some time to think and that means I need time away from you."

"No problem," he said and raised his hands in a gesture of defeat. "If my presence bothers you, I won't walk with you, I'll just saunter along behind you," he said, then grinned. "Besides, you've got a nice back view."

She had no idea why he felt the need to be here at all. Rather than ask him, she whirled around and headed for the hospital, painfully conscious of him walking several paces behind her.

From the moment he'd appeared in her office the

day before, she felt as if her life had spun crazily out of control, and she didn't like it. She knew she had to make a decision about going to California, but she found rational thought next to impossible when Kevin was around.

She was a devoted doctor, in control of her surroundings. She was strong and independent, but when with Kevin, he somehow reminded her that she was a woman besides being a doctor.

She rounded a corner next to an abandoned building, her thoughts filled with Kevin. Out of the corner of her eye, she saw a flash of movement as somebody shot out of the shadows and grabbed her.

The attack was so swift, so unexpected, she didn't have time to scream, she didn't have time to do anything. She fell to the sidewalk. Pain. It shot through her as he followed her down to the ground, his weight crashing on top of her, forcing her breath from her lungs.

His breath was hot and fetid and his hands ripped and tore at the skin of her neck. She fought him, trying to scratch his face and knee him in the stomach.

His face was a contorted mask of rage as he grappled with her. Somewhere in the back of her terror-laden mind, she catalogued his features, knowing somehow it was important that she remember what he look like.

"Hey!"

Phoebe nearly sobbed in relief as she heard Kevin's shout. The man on top of her jumped up and took off running as Kevin raced to her side.

"Phoebe, are you all right?" He knelt down beside her and helped her to a sitting position.

She shook her head. "He...he came out of the building and just jumped on me." She rubbed her neck and felt the welts his fingernails had caused. Her hip ached where she had hit the ground with such force.

"You're hurt," he said, his blue eyes filled with anger. He started to scoop her up in his arms, but she stopped him.

"No, really, I'm fine. I'm just sore." And scared beyond any fear she had ever experienced before.

He looked at her for a long moment. "Are you sure you're all right?"

She forced a smile. "I'm a doctor, I'd know if I was really hurt."

He stood and carefully helped her to her feet and when he pulled her against his chest and wrapped his arms around her, she didn't fight him. Instead, she leaned into his strength and closed her eyes for just a moment.

"I was afraid something like this might happen," he murmured, as if speaking more to himself than to her.

She stepped away from him and looked at him. "What do you mean?"

"I was hoping that last night's break-in at your place was just a coincidence."

"But now you don't think it was?" A new fear iced the blood in her veins as she saw the worry that darkened his eyes.

"No, I don't think it was," he said. His gaze held hers intently. "I think maybe I wasn't the only one looking for you, and in finding you, I've brought danger into your life."

Chapter Three

Kevin sat on a stone bench just outside the hospital's main entrance, waiting for Phoebe to exit the building. Dusk was falling and she'd called him on his cell phone moments before to let him know she was on her way out.

After the attack on her that morning, he'd tried to talk her into going back to her apartment and not working that day, but she'd insisted otherwise.

However, she had agreed to call the police, and she and Kevin and one of Kansas City's finest had sat in her office as she'd given an account of the attack and a description of her attacker. They had agreed not to tell the police what had brought Kevin to Phoebe in the first place. Kevin was afraid it would only complicate matters.

Kevin had given a description of the car the attacker had jumped into at the end of the block, a car that had apparently been waiting for him.

After the officer had left, Phoebe had shooed Kevin away, insisting that what she needed more than anything was to get back to work.

Reluctantly he'd left her, assuming she would be safe surrounded by co-workers, then he had spent much of the day trying to get answers. Unfortunately, he'd managed to gain very few.

Even though he'd been relatively certain that Phoebe would be safe that day at work, when she walked out of the building he was glad to see her, although she looked stressed and exhausted.

"Bad day?" he asked.

"No worse than usual," she said as he guided her toward where his car was parked in the lot.

He frowned as he noted the red marks that still marred the creamy skin of her throat. "Did you put something on those?" he asked.

"Yes, I used half a bottle of antiseptic and I used heat and ice on my hip, which is now sporting a bruise the size of a large grapefruit."

Kevin frowned, momentarily feeling like a heel as he was gifted with a mental flash of a long shapely leg. He opened the passenger door for her and she slid in, wincing slightly.

Frustration, along with a healthy dose of anger swept through him as he thought of the attack on her.

If only he'd been following her more closely, if only he hadn't allowed her to get out of his sight for a single moment.

After he'd left her apartment the night before, he'd had a bad feeling in his gut, a feeling that had prompted him to sleep in the car outside of her building.

"Other than the obvious, are you feeling all right?"

She nodded. "A little jumpy, but okay." She glanced at him curiously. "You didn't sleep in your car last night because you wanted to save money on a hotel bill, did you? You thought something might happen, didn't you?"

"My instincts told me it was possible, but I was hoping my instincts were wrong."

He got into the driver seat and put the key into the ignition, then turned to face her once again. "I've spent the day trying to figure out what in the heck is going on."

She looked at him, her expression vulnerable, her gaze intent. "And what have you figured out?"

He started the engine, then gazed at her once again. "I wish I could tell you exactly what is happening and why, but I can't."

"That man this morning...I think he was after my necklace." She fumbled with the chain inside her smock and grasped the charm in her palm.

"That's the conclusion I reached the minute I saw the scratches on your neck," he said. "And I think it's possible whoever broke into your apartment last night was also looking for the necklace.'' He pulled out of the parking space and headed toward her apartment building.

''But, why? What does the necklace mean? It's been with me for as long as I can remember. Why would somebody be after it now?''

Kevin tightened his grip on the steering wheel. ''Like I told you this morning right after the attack, I think maybe I brought this to your doorstep. When I found you, I found the necklace for somebody else.''

''Who is this Loucan who hired you?'' she asked as she tucked the necklace once again into her smock. ''How do we know he isn't the one behind all this?''

Kevin didn't answer until he'd parked his car at the curb in front of her building. He shut off the engine, then turned to face her. ''I don't think Loucan had anything to do with the attacks on you. I hadn't contacted him to let him know I'd found you when these attacks occurred.'' He gestured toward the building. ''Can we finish this conversation inside your place?''

She hesitated only a moment, then nodded. ''Of course.''

Kevin had a feeling she was a person who didn't particularly like to share her personal space. He knew from her neighbors that she didn't have visitors and even though she'd agreed to allow him in, the agreement had been given with a bit of reluctance.

As they rode up in the elevator, she released a deep

sigh. "Why is it I get the feeling that what happened last night and what happened this morning is just the beginning?"

He wished he could tell her she was overreacting, but he couldn't, nor was he going to give her any false assurances that her life would now return to normal. "Unfortunately, I can't tell you that your feeling is wrong."

They stepped out of the elevator and entered her apartment. He was vaguely surprised to see that all the mess of the night before was gone. And just as he'd suspected, she seemed to be an immaculate housekeeper.

"You must have been up half the night cleaning up," he said, gazing around the room with interest.

Now that the clutter was gone, he could see that the room was decorated in warm colors of dark blue and burgundy, but there was a certain sterility.

Again he was struck by the fact that there were no personal artifacts, no pictures, or knickknacks sitting around. The furniture was tasteful, the place was clean, but it could have belonged to anyone.

"I had trouble sleeping until the mess was cleaned up," she replied and motioned him toward the sofa. "Please, make yourself at home."

"I'd have trouble realizing somebody had searched my place," he said. "It always looks pretty much like yours did last night."

"So, not only are you a good private investigator, you're telling me you're also a slob?"

He grinned. "Yeah, I guess that's what I'm telling you."

She self-consciously ran a hand down the pants of her uniform. "If you don't mind, I'd like to change clothes real quick."

He nodded and took a seat on the sofa. "Go do what you need to do. I'm fine right here."

She disappeared into the bedroom and closed the door behind her. Kevin settled back on the sofa, fighting against a wave of exhaustion that momentarily threatened to overtake him.

He hadn't gotten much sleep the night before. The confines of an economy rental car weren't exactly conducive to comfort, and in any case, he'd been too wound up to sleep and had wanted to keep an eye on things.

He sat up straight as she re-entered the room, clad in a pair of gray sweatpants and a moss-green T-shirt that made her eyes appear a darker, deeper green. "Would you like something to drink?" she asked as she walked into the kitchen area. "Maybe some coffee?"

"Coffee sounds wonderful," he responded. "How long have you lived here?"

"I've been here for the past three years," she said as she made the coffee.

"It isn't exactly the kind of place you'd expect a successful surgeon to be living in."

She flashed him a quick smile. "I'm comfortable here and really haven't seen the need to move. I'm walking distance to the hospital and spend most of my time there anyway."

He liked that about her, that she apparently made personal decisions based on what made her comfortable rather than worrying about presenting a picture of affluence.

As the scent of fresh-brewed coffee filled the room, they spoke for a few minutes about the neighborhood and Kansas City in general.

It wasn't until they were both seated on the sofa with coffee cups in hand that they got back to the matter at hand.

"You mentioned earlier that you don't think this Loucan is behind the attacks on me," she said.

He took a sip of the strong coffee and nodded. "Loucan only knew that I was following a lead when I left California yesterday morning. I didn't tell him where exactly I was headed and I hadn't yet contacted him to tell him I'd found you."

"Did you contact him today?"

"Yeah, I called him right after I left you at the hospital this morning. I've been given an additional assignment where you are concerned."

Her eyes blinked in surprise. "And what's that?"

"Not only am I supposed to get you to Santa Barbara, but I'm to get you there safe and sound. Loucan doesn't want anything happening to you or to your necklace.''

She set her cup down on a coaster on the coffee table, a frown dancing between her eyebrows. ''What is so important about my necklace?''

''I wish I could tell you,'' he replied. He set his cup down as well. ''Do you mind if I look at it?''

She hesitated a long moment, then pulled the charm from her blouse, removed the chain from her neck and handed it to him.

Kevin studied the charm closely. There was no question about it, it was an odd piece. ''Do you know what the symbols and strange writing on it means?''

She shook her head, her pretty blond hair swirling momentarily around her shoulders. ''Not a clue.''

''You mentioned that the charm had been with you for years.''

''Apparently it was around my neck when I was first brought into the hospital. Through the years I've simply bought longer chains to put it on.''

''It's amazing you've kept it all these years,'' he said as he returned it to her.

She gazed down at the charm in her hand, giving him a view of her beautifully long lashes. She looked back up at him, her expression unreadable. ''It was the most important possession I had, the only thing I owned that I believed might have been given to me by some member of my family.'' She pulled the chain back over her head. "So, who do you think wants it and why?"

"I can't begin to guess the why," he said truthfully. "And specifically I don't know the who. I tried to get answers out of Loucan, but he insisted that he would try to explain everything to us when we get to California."

He picked up his coffee cup once again. "What I think has happened is that somebody has been hunting for you besides Loucan...somebody who maybe has been watching me and my movements." He frowned. "And I've brought them right to your doorstep."

"So, what are we going to do?" Her gaze once again held his intently and he was vaguely surprised at the sense of responsibility that swept through him where she was concerned.

"I think the answer to that question lies with you," he replied. "I don't know what I stirred up by finding you, but the man who seems to have at least some of the answers is in California, and he's not talking until we see him face-to-face."

She leaned her head back and closed her eyes, giving him a perfect view of the soft curve of her jawline and the graceful column of her neck.

Kevin knew she was contemplating a trip to California, and more than anything, he wanted her to agree to go with him. He had several reasons for wanting her to do so.

Initially he'd wanted her to go because Loucan had promised him a generous payoff when he delivered any of the four siblings there. All that day, that particular reason for wanting to see her to California had been overwhelmed by a greater need...the need to get some answers.

And now, gazing at her, smelling the sweet floral scent of her and remembering how she'd felt so briefly in his arms that morning, he realized yet another reason for getting her to California. Maybe he was overreacting, but he had a feeling her very life depended on it.

For as long as Phoebe could remember, she'd had a clear sense of purpose and an order to her life. In the blink of Kevin Cartwright's gorgeous blue eyes, all of it seemed to have disintegrated.

The idea of going anywhere near the coast terrified her. The recurring bad dream that haunted her sleep far too often was always about the ocean. Still, the idea of sending Kevin on his way and attempting to continue her life seemed as impossible as her facing the images from her nightmares.

She opened her eyes and looked at him, wondering how it was possible that she trusted so completely a man she'd known for just a little over twenty-four hours. Maybe it was because she had nobody else in her life. She shoved that disturbing thought aside.

"It would take me a day or two to clear my schedule,'' she said, thinking out loud as much as talking to him. ''I suppose we could fly out and back in the same day?''

''I don't think that's a good idea.''

''Why not?'' she asked curiously.

Once again he set his cup down on the table and raked a hand through his hair, his blue eyes momentarily reminding her of her nightmare images of a stormy sea. ''As you heard me tell the officer this morning, the man who attacked you on the street got into a car that was waiting for him. That means there's more than one of them. Flying means leaving a paper trail. If you agree to go to California, then I suggest we drive.''

''Drive? But that will take at least several days,'' she protested.

''True, but it will be days that the bad guys don't know where we are.''

Phoebe slowly digested his statement. She knew he was right. At least in a car they would feel as if they had some sort of control.

''Phoebe.'' He surprised her by reaching out and taking one of her hands in his. ''I'm not trying to be a doomsayer, but I don't think this danger to you is going to just go away.''

She gently extracted her hand from his, far too conscious of the electrifying jolt the momentary physical contact had produced. ''I agree,'' she replied. ''And

I really think I have no choice but to go to California and meet with this Loucan."

She reached up and touched the area in the center of her breasts, where the charm snuggled against her skin. "I want some answers and if this Loucan knows about the charm, then he also must know something about my family."

"You said it will take you a day or two to reschedule things at the hospital. Could you be ready to take off first thing Saturday morning?" he asked.

It was insanity. She couldn't believe that she was actually contemplating getting into a car with a virtual stranger to drive across the country. "Yes, I guess I could clear things by then," she agreed.

"Good." He offered her the first real smile since he'd walked into the apartment. "Now, how about we go down to Myrtle's and I'll treat you to dinner?"

The idea of leaving her apartment as she'd done the night before held little appeal. She was exhausted, and more stressed than she could ever remember being in her life. "I really don't feel like going out."

She frowned, thinking of the contents of her refrigerator. "I'd offer to cook something, but I usually eat out or grab something at the hospital, so the cupboards here are pretty bare."

"Then we'll order in. You like pizza?"

She'd thought she wasn't hungry, but the mention of pizza caused a hunger pang to shoot through her stomach. "I love pizza," she said.

"Do you have a favorite place you order from?"

"Belmonico's. The number is on the pad next to the phone." It was odd, for all of her adult life nobody had ever done anything that remotely resembled taking care of her, but at the moment she was all too willing to allow Kevin to take care of the issue of dinner.

He got up from the sofa and moved to the phone on the desk in the corner of the room. "And let me guess...you like some kind of gross vegetable pizza."

The laugh that bubbled out of her came unexpectedly. "What makes you think I like 'gross vegetable' pizza?"

He shrugged his broad shoulders, his eyes no longer stormy seas, but rather the brilliant blue of a cloudless day. "You had vegetable soup last night at Myrtle's and the waitress said you order the same thing all the time. I figured you might be one of those health-conscious meat-haters."

"I am health conscious, but as far as I'm concerned, there's nothing better than a pepperoni pizza."

"Ah, a woman after my own heart," he replied, then picked up the phone and placed the order.

When he was finished, he joined her again on the sofa, sitting closer to her than he'd been before. Phoebe tried to ignore the scent of him, a smell of clean male and the more subtle hint of a pleasant cologne.

She thought of that moment that morning, when he'd helped her off the sidewalk, then had wrapped her in his arms. She'd felt his heartbeat against her own, had fallen into the warmth of his strong embrace and had wondered why standing in his arms had felt so good…so right.

She dismissed the thought from her mind. After all, she had just suffered a trauma and probably would have welcomed an embrace from King Kong.

"Do you have family, Kevin?" she asked, needing to focus on something other than her innermost thoughts.

"Not anymore," he replied and his eyes darkened slightly. "My mother passed away when I was fifteen and my father died a year ago. I've got some aunts and uncles, but nobody I'm really close to."

She picked up her cup from the coffee table and took a sip of the lukewarm brew. "Tell me about the others you've been looking for."

"There isn't a whole lot to tell. As I mentioned before, there are three others besides you that Loucan wants me to find. There's Thalassa who is supposed to be around thirty-three years old, and Saegar who is around thirty-one and finally there's Kai…K-A-I, who's about your age."

"Kai." The name sent a strange yearning through her and she tightened her grip around her coffee cup.

"What?" Kevin leaned closer to her, apparently

seeing that the name had caused a reaction. "Do you remember something?"

"No...no, nothing. The name just...I don't know... seemed somehow familiar for a moment." The strange yearning, that momentary longing the name had evoked was lost, gone beneath her confusion.

Had those emotions been pulled forth from some distant chord of memory, or simply surged because of her incredible need for connection with a family she'd never known?

She looked at Kevin once again. "I would think it would be relatively easy to find these people, their names are certainly not common."

"Those are just their first names. Loucan doesn't know what their last names might be. I've spent the last three years trying to chase down leads, doing Internet searches, anything I can think of to find these people. I only found you because of the news story. I saw your necklace and realized you might be one of the ones I've been searching for."

Before they could discuss anything further, the pizza arrived. Phoebe got out paper plates and sodas and the two of them sat at the small kitchen table opposite each other.

As if by silent, mutual agreement, they kept the dinnertime conversation light, although again Phoebe was struck by how different she and Kevin seemed to be.

He talked about the movies he'd recently seen and she couldn't remember the last time she'd been to a movie. She talked of the books she had read, and he confessed he wasn't much of a reader other than newspapers and magazines.

He surprised her by telling her he was an ex-cop, then delighted her with silly stories of his time first on the police force in Chicago, then of his time as a private investigator.

She wasn't sure she believed the humorous incidents were completely true, but she appreciated the fact that he seemed to be working hard to relax her, to coax some laughter.

But the respite from tension lasted only for the course of their meal. As they worked together to clean up, Phoebe once again was intensely aware of him and the utterly masculine energy that rolled off him.

He set her on edge, with his sexy blue eyes and slightly crooked, but charming smile.

It wasn't until after they had finished cleaning and were once again seated on the sofa that he looked at her somberly. ''What do you think about having a roommate for the next couple of days?''

The question completely caught her off guard. She looked at him in surprise. ''What are you talking about?''

''I checked out of my hotel this afternoon and thought maybe I could bunk here on your sofa until we leave Saturday morning.''

"You were so certain that I would agree to go to California?" she asked, knowing she was being churlish but unable to help her initial emotional response.

"No." His gaze met hers unflinching. "But, I am relatively certain that you are still in danger, and I'd much prefer to be here on your sofa where I can protect you. Of course, I can bunk in my car and watch the front entrance of this building, but that leaves the back and side entrances open to whoever wants to sneak in."

A flush warmed her cheeks and she averted her gaze from his. "I'm sorry, I guess I'm not thinking clearly."

"Apology accepted. I'd say you're allowed to be in a bit of a mental jumble considering all that's happened in the past twenty-four hours."

He reached out and took her hand in his. His gaze darkened as it lingered on her neck, where she knew the fingernail marks were still visible. "Look, Doc, I just want to make sure nothing else bad happens to you. Besides, this sofa definitely feels more comfortable than the driver seat in that rental car."

Again she felt uncomfortable by the fact that his hand felt so good holding hers. She pulled her hand from his and stood. "All right, you can sleep here on the sofa," she agreed.

She was suddenly beyond exhaustion. She'd had little sleep the night before, the trauma of the morning's events, then a full day of work.

Her emotions had gone from the sweet hope of possibly finding members of a long-lost family to the terror of the personal attacks on her and her home. She felt raw and exposed and far too vulnerable to Kevin's masculine charm.

"If you don't mind, I'll just get you a pillow and a blanket, then I'm going on to bed. I'm exhausted," she said.

He nodded and stood as she left the living room and went back into her bedroom. She found a clean set of sheets and a spare blanket in her closet, but had no spare pillow other than one of the two on her bed. She grabbed one of those, then returned to the living room.

He met her in the narrow hallway and took the pillow and blanket from her. "Thanks." His eyes twinkled with a touch of mischief. "Of course, if you really want to get my first-rate kind of protection service, I could sleep in the bed next to you."

"I'll take my chances with your second-rate kind of service…where you sleep on the couch and I sleep in my bed."

He cast her that appealing slightly crooked grin of his. "I figured that was the choice you'd make." His smile fell aside and he placed a hand on her arm, sending rivulets of warmth through her. "Seriously, Doc, sleep well tonight. I promise you nobody will bother you while I'm on the job."

"Thank you, Kevin." She stepped away from the warmth of his hand. "I'll see you in the morning."

She wasn't sure why, but she felt as if she were escaping as she ran into her bedroom and closed the door behind her.

For just a moment, she'd wondered what it would be like to lie in a bed next to Kevin, to fall asleep with the smell of him filling her senses, to feel his body heat radiating next to her.

She had never thought about such things before, but then again she'd never had her apartment broken into or been attacked on the street before.

She changed into her nightgown, shut off the bedroom light and crawled into bed, her thoughts still consumed with the man who was in her living room.

Was it because he might provide a possible link to long-lost family that she was so attracted to him? Or was it something else...some crazy chemistry at work, chemistry that sprang from the notion that at the moment he was protecting her?

It didn't matter what it was, she certainly didn't intend to do anything about it. Other than a crazy three months over a year ago, she'd lived her life so far just fine without a man. She was an independent, strong woman who needed nobody in her life.

Besides, the one thing she had to remember was that to Kevin Cartwright, she was nothing more than a job...nothing more than a paycheck.

Chapter Four

The pillow she'd given him with its pale floral pillowcase smelled of a combination of the scent of her perfume and sleepy femininity.

Kevin sat on the sofa and hugged the pillow to his chest, wondering how she looked sprawled across floral sheets, her hair all tousled and her lips swollen from his kisses.

He frowned and threw the pillow to the side. What he should be thinking about was the cross-country trip they would begin on Saturday morning.

The way he had it figured, if they could drive ten hours a day, they should be able to do the trip within two and a half days, putting them into Santa Barbara sometime Monday afternoon.

There was a hotel not far from the wharf where

Kevin usually met Loucan. It wasn't exactly five-star accommodations, but he could check them in under a false name and hopefully they would be safe.

He also would have to try to trade his rental car for another one, knowing that whoever was watching him would probably already have his license number and make and model of the vehicle.

He stood and made up the sofa with the sheets and blanket, his mind whirling with question after question. Who was after Phoebe? What was it about the necklace that made it worth stealing?

Even if it were made of pure silver, which he didn't think it was, the weight was so light it couldn't be worth more than a couple hundred bucks at the most. Certainly not worth all the trouble somebody seemed to be going to in order to gain possession of it.

He eyed the makeshift bed, deciding there was no way he could crawl into it before taking a shower. Surely Phoebe wouldn't mind if he made himself at home and used her shower.

The bathroom was decorated in light pastels. The shower curtain was a floral design and the towels and soap dish were a pale pink.

He left the door to the bathroom cracked open, not wanting any surprises while he took a quick shower. He opened the closet and found clean towels neatly folded on one of the shelves. Another shelf held an array of bottles and lotions, shampoo and makeup.

He picked up one of the perfume bottles, uncapped

it and took a sniff, a wave of pleasure sweeping through him at the flowery scent. It smelled of Phoebe.

What in the heck was he doing? Standing in front of a bathroom closet sniffing perfume? He grabbed a towel and closed the closet door, then turned on the water in the shower. He unstrapped his gun from his ankle and placed it on the counter, then quickly stripped off his clothes.

It was the fastest shower he'd ever taken as he didn't want to be too long beneath the water where sounds from the apartment were muted.

As always, the first place he washed was his chest, where a ropy scar began just under his breastbone and extended in a jagged line down the length of his abdomen. He rarely thought about the old scar, only knew that it required that he always wear a shirt because it was gruesome.

When he was finished with his shower, he dried off and pulled on his clothes, wishing he'd thought to bring in his suitcase from the trunk of his car before Phoebe had gone to bed.

He left the bathroom, but paused in the hallway and listened for a moment in an attempt to become familiar with the normal sounds of the apartment.

It was the time of year where no heating or air cooling was necessary, so there was no sound of vents popping and crackling. In fact, he was vaguely surprised at the utter silence of the place.

Returning to the living room, he thought again of the woman he was now supposed to protect and get to California. Was Phoebe telling him the truth about everything? Did she genuinely not know why her necklace was important to somebody?

She'd seemed genuinely perplexed, but Kevin had been a cop and a private investigator long enough to recognize that the world was filled with good liars.

He shucked his jeans and shirt, and clad only in a pair of boxers, sank onto the sofa. With the gun in easy reach on the coffee table, he willed himself to relax. The sheets smelled of fabric softener and the pillow smelled of her. These were his last conscious thoughts.

He awoke suddenly, unsure what exactly had pulled him from his sleep. The apartment was still dark, although it was not the profound darkness of middle of the nighttime hours. He didn't move and held his breath, listening for any telltale sound that didn't belong to the place.

Coffee. That's what had awakened him. The scent of fresh-brewed coffee filled the air. Unless somebody had broken in due to caffeine deprivation, he assumed Phoebe had made the brew.

He sat up and squinted at the luminous dial of his wristwatch. Five o'clock. He couldn't remember the last time he'd been up so early.

Grabbing his jeans, he stood and yanked them on,

noticing that a light shone from beneath the bathroom door. He pulled on his shirt, then padded barefoot into the kitchen and pulled two cups from the cabinets.

He'd just poured coffee into the cups and set them on the table when she appeared, dressed in a pair of black slacks and a black and gray striped blouse.

"Some watchdog you are," she exclaimed when she saw him. "I showered and dressed and made coffee and you didn't twitch a muscle."

He gestured to the coffee he'd poured for her and sat at the table. "Trust me, had you made a noise that was an abnormal one, I'd have been at your defense in a second."

She sat across from him and pulled her cup toward her. "You lied to me," she said.

He looked at her in surprise. "Lied about what?"

A smile curved one corner of her mouth. "You don't snore only when sleeping on your back. When I came through to make the coffee you were on your side and you were snoring up a storm."

Kevin was surprised to feel a slight edge of embarrassment rise up inside him. "The air must be unusually dry in here," he said gruffly. "And please, tell me why you're up at this ungodly hour of the morning."

The smile that had momentarily lifted her lips disappeared. "I'm an early riser, Kevin, obviously quite different than you. Besides, I need to get to work early today and start working on rearranging my schedule and making sure my patients will be cared for while we're gone to California."

He nodded. "I noticed last night that you have a computer. Are you on the Internet?"

"Yes, why?"

"If you don't mind I'd like to spend a little time on it while you're at work."

She frowned. "You mean while I'm at work you'll be here?"

"Well, yeah...unless you expected me to spend the day in my car."

Her cheeks flushed prettily and he noticed how the dark shades of her blouse made her hair look more blond. "I guess I just hadn't given it any thought," she finally said.

"Look, I know you're not accustomed to having anyone here and I promise while you're gone I won't snoop around." He grinned. "I won't even take a single peek into your underwear drawer."

She took a sip of her coffee, her gaze meeting his over the rim of her cup. "I don't find you half as amusing as you apparently find yourself," she said as she set her cup back down on the table.

"That's all right," he agreed easily. "I find myself amusing enough for the both of us."

She didn't crack a smile, but rather looked at her wristwatch. "I'd really like to go ahead and get to work," she said.

She carried her cup to the sink, washed it out, then

placed it back in the cabinet and turned to face him expectantly.

Kevin got up and went into the living room where he quickly strapped on his gun, then slipped on his loafers. The woman definitely didn't seem to have much of a sense of humor, he thought. She was so uptight she should squeak when she walked.

Moments later they were in his car headed for the hospital. "Call me when you're ready to come home and I'll come and get you," he said as he pulled up in front of the building.

"All right." She opened her car door and stepped out, then leaned back in, a twinkle lighting her eyes. "I'll save you the trouble," she said. "White cotton bikinis…very boring."

With these words, she shut the door and headed for the building. It took Kevin a moment to realize she was talking about her underwear, and he chuckled. Perhaps he had underestimated her sense of humor.

As he pulled away from the curb his mind granted him a revised image of her stretched out on a bed with flowered sheets. In this vision she was clad only in a pair of white cotton bikinis, but there was nothing remotely boring about them.

It was another long day, made longer by the knowledge that Kevin was in her apartment. What was starting to make her nervous was the fact that with each minute that passed in his company, she trusted him more.

Trusting anyone didn't come easily to Phoebe. She'd learned early in life as a foster child that people couldn't be trusted. Could Kevin?

It wasn't as if he'd been drawn to her by some magical force or chemical attraction. He'd been paid to find her and she was certain there was a reward awaiting him at the end of the trip to California.

She told herself she'd be a fool to trust a man she'd known for such a short period of time, but she couldn't help but be glad to see him when she exited the hospital at the end of the day.

For the first time in years, she truly didn't want to go home to a silent, empty apartment.

"Hey, Doc." He greeted her with a warm smile as she slid into the passenger seat of his car. "You look beat."

"Gee, thanks," she replied dryly.

"Let me rephrase that. You look beautiful, but beat."

"I am tired," she said. He, on the other hand looked freshly showered and shaved and far too handsome for her emotional comfort.

He wore a pair of tight jeans and a navy T-shirt that deepened the hue of his eyes to an impossible blue. Without the distraction of whiskers, his facial features appeared sharper, more cleanly defined.

"You've told me about your work, but you haven't

said much about your personal life,'' she said, suddenly curious about the man who had the job of protecting her against some unidentifiable danger.

''What would you like to know?'' he asked as he pulled away from the hospital.

''Have you ever been married?''

''Never.''

''But I'll bet you've had lots of girlfriends.''

''Hundreds...maybe thousands.''

She could tell he was teasing her by the mischievous grin that touched his lips. ''I'm serious, Kevin. Do you have a special somebody in your life?''

''Nah. I haven't really dated anyone seriously in the last five years.'' He rubbed a hand across his chest, then returned it to the steering wheel. ''What about you? You do a lot of dating?''

She wanted to tell him yes, that half a dozen doctors at the hospital were madly in love with her and she was exhausted each day from fielding all their advances. Instead she answered honestly. ''I rarely date. There just never seems to be enough hours in the day.''

''Ah, but you should always make time for romance,'' he replied as he parked the car outside her building.

She wasn't sure she believed that he hadn't dated anyone in the past five years. Kevin was too much of an extrovert, too charming of a man to spend his nights alone.

The moment she entered the apartment, she was greeted by the scent of fresh garlic and simmering tomatoes. "You cooked?"

"I figured you probably hadn't had a real, home-cooked meal in a long time," he said as he headed for the kitchen. "The home-cooked down at Myrtle's doesn't count. I hope you like Italian."

"I love it." The idea that he'd cooked because he thought she would appreciate home-cooking touched her deeply. She thought it just might be one of the nicest things anyone had ever done for her.

"Why don't you go change into something comfortable and I'll boil the pasta," he suggested.

Moments later, as she changed into a pair of jogging pants and an oversized T-shirt, she tried not to let Kevin's kindness affect her too much. He'd probably cooked because he wanted to eat something other than take-out or Myrtle's fare.

When she entered the kitchen, he was stirring a pot of boiling macaroni. He pointed to a glass of red wine sitting on the counter. "Sit down and have some wine and I'll have it on the table in just a few minutes."

"Isn't there anything I can do?"

He smiled at her. "I'd say you've put in enough hours today to earn somebody waiting on you a little bit. Sit down and enjoy."

A sudden sting of tears burned at her eyes and she quickly sat down at the table and picked up the glass of wine. Nobody had ever noticed how many hours she put in or how exhausted she was, and his caring both surprised and touched her.

Take care, Phoebe Jones, a tiny voice whispered in the back of her mind. He's here because you have a charm that somebody wants and he's being paid handsomely to be here.

"So, you're a good private investigator, a slob in your home, a snorer at night, and you cook," she observed.

"I cook well," he replied. "And I figure that counters the slob and snoring aspect of my personality." He carried the pot of boiling spaghetti noodles to the sink where he emptied it into a colander.

"Have you always liked to cook?" she asked, then took a sip of her wine.

"I didn't really start until I was fifteen when my mother died. It didn't take me long to realize my father had no clue exactly what a kitchen was used for." He paused a moment to rinse the noodles, then poured them into an awaiting serving bowl.

"Anyway, I took a home-economics course and discovered I truly loved to cook." He spooned the thick, savory-smelling sauce over the spaghetti and placed the bowl on the table. He grabbed a colorful salad from the refrigerator and a loaf of Italian bread from the stove, then joined her at the table.

"Wow, I'm impressed," she said. And she was. Cooking had certainly never been one of her strengths.

"Ah, this is nothing," he replied, but it was obvious he was pleased. "I take it you don't do much cooking," he said as he passed her the salad.

"If it wasn't for Myrtle's, I'd have starved long ago," she confessed.

"It takes all kinds. I wouldn't want to be in a world where there were no surgeons," he said.

She smiled at him, relaxing by the moment. "And I wouldn't want to be in a world where there were no cooks."

They were silent for a few minutes as they filled their plates. "So, how was your day at work?" he asked when they'd started eating.

"Busy, as usual, but I've almost managed to get my schedule clear for the next couple of weeks. This sauce is heavenly."

"Thanks. How's little Michael doing?"

"He's not one of my patients, but he's quickly become one of the favorites of the hospital." Phoebe thought of the brave little boy. "It's too soon to tell how much use he'll have of his arm, but we're hoping he'll have some partial use."

"It must be great to be a part of something that puts people back together again," he said.

She nodded and frowned. "Unfortunately, not all the surgery stories are happy ones."

"But we don't have to discuss that now. Good food calls for pleasant conversation."

The food was wonderful and the conversation just

as good as they enjoyed the meal. Kevin was easy to talk to, opinionated and not afraid to share his opinions. But he also seemed more than willing to listen to opposing opinions.

As they cleaned up after the meal, Phoebe tried to avoid physical contact with him, but in the small confines of the kitchen it was next to impossible.

Their shoulders bumped and their fingers met as he rinsed the dishes and she placed them in the dishwasher. She couldn't help but notice that he had nice hands, with broad fingers and neatly trimmed nails.

For just a moment, she wondered what his hands would feel like trailing down the length of her body. Would he be as thoughtful as a lover as he was as a houseguest?

Appalled by her inappropriate thoughts, she shoved them firmly and resolutely out of her head. She'd be crazy to even think about any kind of a relationship with Kevin. Not only did they have little in common, she knew once they reached California and his job was done, he'd go back to his life and she'd return to hers.

When they had the kitchen cleaned, she made coffee and they carried their cups into the living room and sat on the sofa, him at one end, her at the other.

"Besides grocery shopping and cooking a wonderful meal, what else did you do today?" she asked.

"I spent most of the day surfing the Internet."

"Looking for the three other people you're supposed to find?"

"That, and researching something else." He placed his cup on the coffee table, then put his hand in his pocket and withdrew what appeared to be an old gold coin. "Loucan gave me this as a payment about six months ago and since that time I've been trying to figure out where it came from."

"Can I see it?" She placed her cup next to his then leaned closer to him to take the coin he proffered to her. She eyed it curiously. "It looks like real gold," she said.

"Oh, it's solid gold," he replied. "You can see on the face there's a picture of a woman."

"The writing looks Spanish."

"It is. I found a reference to it today, but what I found out makes no sense."

"So, what did you find out?" She gave him back the coin.

"Come here and I'll show you." He stood and walked over to the built-in desk that held her computer. He motioned her into the chair, then leaned over her to maneuver the mouse.

She tried to ignore the heat that emanated from his body, searing through hers at each point of contact. She also tried not to think about the sexy male scent that drifted from him.

He pulled up a Web page that showed a drawing

of the coin he'd shown her. There was a description of the coin at the bottom of the page.

She read the text, then looked up at him, confused by what she'd just read. "I don't understand, according to this these coins were made specifically for a celebration of Queen Isabella but were lost at sea when the ship was taken by pirates and later lost at sea in a storm."

He nodded. "If you're confused, then don't feel all alone."

He logged off the computer and they returned to the sofa. She sat where she had before, but instead of returning to his own corner of the sofa, he sat right next to her. He placed the coin on the coffee table, a frown wrinkling his forehead. "If these coins were only made for a specific celebration years and years ago and were lost at sea, then how did Loucan come to have one in his possession?"

"Don't tell me," she exclaimed. "The good news is you might have found a member of my family. The bad news is he might be a sea scavenger...a pirate."

"Hey, we don't know for sure," he said, apparently hearing the touch of misery in her voice. He reached out and took her hand in his. "For all we know, Loucan is a very respectable businessman and was given this coin for one reason or another."

She knew he'd said the words to appease her, but she also knew he didn't positively believe his own words. She also knew she should pull her hand from the warmth of his, but she didn't.

Instead she released a deep, long sigh. "When I was younger and still had hopes of someday finding family, I wondered if I'd be happy with what I found. One minute I was a princess sent away for my own protection, and the next minute I'd wonder if my parents were felons, or drug addicts, or simply people who just didn't want me."

He squeezed her hand, his blue eyes radiating an all-encompassing warmth. "The not knowing must be tough."

She finally pulled her hand from his, self-consciously aware of his nearness. "Tell me about your parents," she said.

He leaned back and frowned thoughtfully. "My mother was a quiet woman, but it was a comforting quiet. She was very loving, a truly good woman." He was silent for a moment and Phoebe thought she could feel the pain that memories of his mother had evoked.

"I think it must be more difficult to love a parent, then lose them rather than never know them at all," she said softly.

"Perhaps," he agreed. "Although with knowing exactly who your parents are, there aren't any questions. If you have good parents you're lucky, if you have bad parents you endure."

"And what about your father?"

His eyes darkened just a touch. "My father was a tough guy, an ex-marine turned cop. He was loud, dictatorial, and I respected and loved him a lot." He paused again and Phoebe remained silent, sensing there was more to come.

He raked a hand through his hair and sat forward in the seat, his body filled with a sudden tension. "Unfortunately, my dad and I had a falling out when I decided to leave the police department, so when he died we weren't speaking to each other."

She felt his pain, as sharp and internal as if it were her own. "I'm so sorry, Kevin," she said softly and placed her hand on his forearm.

She felt the tension leaving him, but when he turned his head to look at her again his eyes were still darker than normal.

Without warning, he leaned forward and touched her lips with his own in a sweet, gentle kiss. But there was nothing sweet or gentle in her response to the kiss. Fever swept through her, burning her with a sensual heat and she found herself eagerly responding.

He apparently recognized her positive response and sought to deepen the kiss, touching his tongue to the bottom of her upper lip, then sliding just inside her mouth.

At the same time his arms surrounded her, subtly pulling her closer to him, and she wanted to be closer to him. She wanted to feel the breadth of his chest against her breasts, his heartbeat pounding against her own. She wanted it so badly it frightened her and she pulled away from him and jumped up from the sofa.

"You shouldn't have done that," she said, her voice half-breathless.

One corner of his lips moved upward in a half smile. "I have trouble fighting my impulses and I definitely had an impulse to kiss you."

"You mustn't do it again," she exclaimed. "And I think it's time I call it a night."

He smiled indulgently. "Escaping?"

She felt her cheeks warm. "Don't be ridiculous. I'm just tired, that's all. I'll see you in the morning."

He nodded. She started down the hallway toward her room but paused as he called her name. She turned back to face him.

"Doc, it was just one little, simple kiss."

"Of course, that's all it was," she agreed, then turned and entered the privacy of her bedroom.

She closed her bedroom door and leaned against it for a long moment, replaying the taste, the texture, the sensation of his lips against hers.

What he didn't seem to understand was that there had been nothing little or simple about that kiss.

Chapter Five

He shouldn't have kissed her. As Kevin placed her suitcase next to his in the trunk of the rental car on Saturday morning, he chastised himself for kissing Phoebe on Thursday night.

She had just started to loosen up a little, then he'd followed through on his impulse to kiss her and she'd tightened up more taut than a string on a violin.

She'd worked late the night before and when they'd returned to the apartment, they'd discussed their plans to leave this morning and nothing more. She'd been cool and distant and had immediately escaped into the privacy of her bedroom.

He slammed the trunk closed, then absently rubbed the scar on his chest through the thin T-shirt he wore. It wasn't like he wanted a relationship with Phoebe.

He'd long ago decided that the love and marriage route wasn't for him. He'd just wanted to steal a kiss from a pretty woman.

What he hadn't counted on was how hot her mouth would be against his, how sweet the taste of her lips, and how much he would want to repeat the pleasure.

But he wouldn't. He'd known Phoebe long enough to know that she deserved a real man, a whole man, not some scarred-up coward who hadn't even been able to earn his own father's respect.

He turned as the door to the apartment building opened and she came out, looking beautiful in a pair of jeans and a white cotton short-sleeved blouse. "What's that for?" he asked, pointing to the raincoat draped over her arm and the umbrella she held in one hand.

"It's going to rain before the day is over."

He frowned. "According to the weatherman last night, it's supposed to be clear all weekend."

She shrugged. "It doesn't matter what the weatherman said. It's going to rain."

"If you say so," he replied dubiously. "All set to go?"

She nodded and together they got into the car. "I still don't see why you wanted to start so late," she said once they were in the car and he was pulling away from the curb. "We're going to be right in the middle of rush-hour traffic."

"I don't mind the traffic," he replied. There was a

specific reason he'd wanted to start their trip during morning traffic. It was easier to lose a tail when darting in and around other cars, but he didn't want to worry her with that bit of information.

He drove at a leisurely pace down the side streets that would take them to the interstate, glancing in his rearview mirror often to see if a tail appeared.

It took only two turns to realize that they'd picked up a white sedan. The car was far enough back that Kevin couldn't see the occupants and he wasn't positive that it was following them or simply headed in the same direction as them.

He shot a glance at Phoebe, who appeared somewhat relaxed, her gaze focused out the front window. "Did you sleep well?" he asked.

"Not really," she admitted after a moment of hesitation. "To be honest, I'm pretty nervous about this whole thing."

He shot her a quick smile. "I'd worry about you if you weren't nervous. This is a big step, driving cross-country to find out about your roots."

She nodded and resumed a thoughtful stare out the window.

As they hit the entrance to the interstate, Kevin focused entirely on the traffic and the car behind him. Blatantly aggressive, he nosed his way out into the traffic, earning a finger salute and a honk from the man driving the car he cut off.

Traffic was moving at a fairly quick pace, but

Kevin moved quicker, zigzagging from lane to lane. He heard Phoebe's gasp and from the corner of his eye saw her fingers gripping the ends of the armrests.

Still, he shot from the left to the right, then back to the left lane, earning the ire of the drivers around him. He kept his concentration focused on the traffic and his rearview mirror. The white sedan mirrored his movements, confirming to him that they were, indeed, being followed.

He increased his speed and his evasive driving, satisfied when he could no longer see the white sedan behind them. An exit ramp approached and he zoomed across from the left-hand lane and took the exit on the right amid honking horns and squealing tires.

At the bottom of the ramp he ran through the stop sign and took a right-hand turn on two wheels. ''Stop this car,'' Phoebe gasped angrily.

''Hang on.'' He pulled into a gas station and drove around the back of the building, nosing his car around the side and placing it where he had a visual of the cars passing by the station.

''Are you insane?'' She opened her car door and started to get out, but before she could he reached over and grabbed her arm.

''Stay in the car,'' he said firmly.

''Let go of me,'' she said, her eyes blazing green fire. ''You're a lunatic.''

''We were being followed.''

His words doused the flames in her eyes and she breathed a deep sigh and shut the door once again. ''You should have told me,'' she exclaimed.

''I didn't want you to be concerned.''

A flash of fire lit her eyes once again. ''And you thought that kind of driving wouldn't concern me?'' she accused.

Again she drew a deep breath, as if to steady her nerves and control her anger. ''Kevin, you have to tell me what's going on. Please don't try to protect me by not telling me things. I need to know the truth at all times.''

''All right, it's a deal. The truth and nothing but the truth is what you'll get.'' He put the car into drive and eased away from the side of the gas station. When he reached the road he turned away from the interstate.

''We're going to take side streets and return to the place where I rented this car.''

''Why?''

He smiled patiently. ''Because the people who are attempting to tail us obviously know this car. I've arranged for another one to be ready for us.''

''You knew we'd be followed?''

''I wasn't sure, but if I were trying to get an opportunity to rip that necklace off your neck, I'd be following us.''

She pulled the charm from inside her blouse and

gripped it in her hand. "I just can't figure out why this is so important."

Kevin frowned. "Hopefully when we get to California, Loucan will have some answers for us."

It took them fifteen minutes to get back to the car rental agency, then another fifteen to get situated in the black sports car. It was almost eight-thirty by the time they got back on the road.

They traveled in silence, Kevin once again watching his rearview mirror for a potential tail. Finally, after an hour of seeing nothing suspicious, he began to relax.

He glanced at Phoebe, noting how the morning sunshine played in the strands of her blond hair. If he ever decided to get involved with a woman, it would be a woman with hair like hers, filled with sunshine and sweet smelling.

Of course, he had no intention of getting into a relationship with any woman. It had been over five years since he'd dated anyone seriously.

"Why did you quit the police department?" she asked.

He looked at her in surprise. "What brought that up?"

"I don't know. After the demonstration of your driving skills, I was just wondering."

He'd said that from here on out he'd tell her the truth, but he hadn't promised to bare his soul, pick at his scars. "I was ready for a change," he said as his mind worked to come up with a logical reason. "Basically, I wanted to be my own boss so I could be lazy whenever I felt like it."

She gazed at him askance. "Was your father a Chicago cop, too?"

"Yeah." Kevin felt his hands tightening on the steering wheel at thoughts of his father. "Although we were in different departments. He was a homicide detective and I worked vice."

A small smile curved her lips. "Somehow that doesn't surprise me."

He laughed, recognizing that whenever she smiled he wanted to kiss her again...and again. Kissing her had definitely been a mistake. Now that he knew the pleasure it brought, he wanted to repeat it.

Frowning, he once again focused all his attention on the road ahead. He didn't want to think about kissing her and he definitely didn't want to think about his father. His father had died deeply disappointed by Kevin.

He didn't intend to allow Phoebe to know him well enough to be disappointed in him and he certainly didn't intend to hang around her long enough for her to realize he was nothing but a coward.

Phoebe didn't know what had happened, but Kevin had withdrawn from her as effectively as if he'd stepped out of the car and gotten on a bus.

Somehow she knew something she had said to him

had caused him to become tense. His hands were wrapped around the steering wheel in a death grip and a knot of muscles in his jaw clenched just beneath the skin.

She remembered him telling her that he and his father had had a falling out and she had a feeling there was more baggage there than he'd pretended.

Leaning her head against the backrest she told herself it was none of her business. The less she knew about Kevin Cartwright, the better.

She had learned a long time ago to keep a bit of distance between herself and everyone else. In her profession it was necessary for emotional survival.

She didn't realize she'd fallen asleep until she jerked awake. It must have been the sound of the windshield wipers swooshing across the window that roused her from her sleep.

Straightening in her seat, she cast a glance at Kevin.

"Have a nice nap?" he asked.

"Yes. How long was I asleep?" She ran her fingers through her hair, hoping she didn't have a case of bed-head.

"About an hour." He gestured toward the window. "You were right about the rain." He shot her a quick glance. "Are you able to do that often?"

"What?"

"Forecast the weather?"

"Usually," she said truthfully.

"Do you have a bum knee that acts up when it's going to rain, or do you get a headache or what?"

"None of the above," she replied. She tried to figure out how to explain to him something she had never understood. "I just seem to be particularly attuned to the weather patterns and changes. I just feel it inside of me."

"Loucan said it was possible the four people I'm looking for might have unusual abilities."

"Unusual abilities?"

"Yeah, I didn't think much about it at the time."

"Well, I don't think of this as an unusual ability," she said. "I think there are lots of people who know when the weather is about to change."

"I'm sure not one of them," he replied. "I get caught in the rain without rain gear on a regular basis."

They fell silent, the only sound the rhythmic cadence of the wipers moving across the window. Phoebe tried to ignore the fact that his presence seemed to fill the small interior of the car.

The scent of him was more than pleasant, and if she focused on it long enough she'd start thinking about the kiss they had shared, and she definitely didn't want to do that.

They drove through a hamburger place for lunch and ate in the car. For the remainder of the afternoon their conversation was casual, mostly about the scenery and points of interest that they passed. They stopped only for gas, both eager to get as many miles behind them as possible.

It was after seven when Kevin pulled into a restaurant on the outskirts of Denver. "I don't know about you, but I don't want another burger gobbled while I'm driving," he said. "Why don't we call it a day. We can eat a nice, leisurely meal then check into that motel." He pointed to the chain motel next to the restaurant.

"Sounds good to me," she said, although a nervous flutter went off in her stomach at the thought of sharing a motel room with him. It was one thing to share an apartment where she had her own room and he slept on the sofa, quite another to share the intimate quarters of a motel room.

Her nervousness only increased as they ate their evening meal. Kevin ordered meat loaf with mashed potatoes and gravy and Phoebe ordered a Caesar chicken salad. He teased her about her choice of a salad and she joked with him about all the cholesterol he was putting into his body.

But even with the teasing tone of the conversation, her nervous anticipation of the night to come increased with every moment that passed.

By the time dinner was finished and they were driving to the motel entrance, her insides were screaming with tension. "I'll check us in. You wait right here with the doors locked," he said as he opened the driver door to exit. "If anything happens, lean on the horn."

She punched down the locks as he left, then watched him saunter toward the motel office door. The man definitely had a walk that promised all kinds of things...things she absolutely didn't want, she reminded herself.

He was back at the car within minutes. She unlocked his door and he slid in behind the wheel once again. "We're in room eight, and at least for tonight we're John and Mary Caldwell."

"You signed us in under a false name?"

"And charged the room on my John Caldwell charge card. Better to be safe than sorry."

"And who is John Caldwell?"

"A buddy of mine in California. I've got his charge card and a spare set of identification. He looks enough like me to be my twin."

"And he doesn't mind that you impersonate him and rack up credit card charges in his name?" she asked incredulously.

He shot her that charming grin of his. "He doesn't mind as long as I pay the credit card charges I rack up in his name." He pulled up in front of the middle of the unit where a door displayed a large gold number eight. "Honey, we're home," he said and opened his car door.

She wished she were home...home in her little apartment, safe within the world she had built for herself, with no mystery surrounding her and no Kevin to tempt her.

At least there were two double beds, she thought with relief as they entered the small room. The room was decorated in normal motel style—gold matching bedspreads, gold heavily lined curtains and a bland landscape painting above each of the beds.

Kevin placed his suitcase on the bed nearest the door, indicating to her that she take the bed next to the wall. "Why don't you shower or do whatever you need to do to get ready for bed, then I will," he said.

"All right." Self-consciously she opened her suitcase and took out the items she would need... nightgown, clean underwear, shampoo, and hairbrush.

As she went into the bathroom, Kevin was deadbolting the door and placing the safety chain on. Moments later she stood beneath a hot drizzle of water, trying to ease muscles that were stiff from travel and perhaps a tad bit of apprehension about the sleeping arrangements.

She showered quickly, knowing Kevin must be exhausted from the day's drive. As she slid on her nightshirt, she wished she had brought a robe with her. At least the nightshirt was a thick pink cotton, and although rather short, left plenty to the imagination.

As she brushed her wet hair, she chided herself for her worries. What made her think Kevin would even notice what her nightshirt looked like? What made her think he would be remotely interested in what was beneath the nightshirt?

Drawing a deep breath, she grabbed her clothes and her brush and left the bathroom. She was grateful that Kevin was digging around in his suitcase and paid no attention to her as she crossed the room.

Taking advantage of his preoccupation, she threw her clothes and brush into her suitcase, placed the suitcase on the floor, then scurried beneath the covers of the bed.

He didn't turn and look at her until she was safely covered from just beneath her chin to the tip of her toes. She watched as he picked up the clock on the nightstand between their beds.

"I'm going to set the alarm for six in the morning," he said, gazing at her for the first time since she'd left the bathroom. "Tomorrow is going to be a long day in the car, so we'd both better get a good night's sleep."

"That sounds good to me," she said and dutifully closed her eyes. A moment later she heard the sound of the shower start and knew he had left the room.

She opened her eyes and stared at the ceiling overhead, trying desperately not to imagine Kevin in the shower. Dressed, he was sexy enough. Undressed she knew he would be devastating.

She could almost imagine his broad chest, covered with a fine coating of brown hair. She could easily imagine how that chest and those springy, soft hairs would feel beneath her fingertips.

As the sound of the shower water stopped, she slammed her eyelids closed again, trying to banish the vision in her head, the tingling of her fingers.

She'd tried the relationship thing once before, with dismal results. Certainly falling into any kind of a relationship with Kevin would be true folly. She was an intelligent, rational woman and didn't intend to make that kind of a mistake.

Turning over on her side, she faced the wall, trying not to think about the one relationship she'd ventured into, a relationship that had ended badly.

She knew the moment he'd left the bathroom. The scent of clean male filled the room. The sounds indicated he was getting into bed and pulling up the covers, then he shut out the nightstand lamp, plunging the room into complete and total darkness.

For a long moment the only sound in the room was the distant noise of car doors slamming outside as other travelers stopped for the night.

"Are you still awake?" his deep voice asked softly.

She thought about not replying and pretending to be asleep, but didn't. "Yes," she replied and turned over once again.

He released a deep sigh. "It always take me a while to unwind and go to sleep."

"Me, too," she admitted.

"You're an easy travel companion."

She smiled in the darkness. "Thanks, you aren't so bad yourself." She hesitated a moment, then propped her elbow beneath her and looked in his direction even though she could see nothing in the profound darkness of the room. "Have you really not seriously dated anyone for the past five years?" she asked.

"Really," he replied, his voice smooth and low.

"Why not?"

He was silent for a long moment and she worriedly wondered if she was prying too closely into his personal life. She was just about to take back the question when he spoke again.

"Right after I quit the police force, I moved to Los Angeles and started my private investigation business. California is a whole different world from Chicago. I was working a lot of hours and building contacts and it was hard to meet available women."

"I can't imagine you having trouble meeting women," she replied. "You're so outgoing, such an extrovert."

"And charming. Don't forget charming," he added.

She laughed. "Okay, and charming."

"What about you, Doc? Do you really not date at all?"

It was strange, there was something both intensely intimate and yet safe in the darkness, making soul-baring a little easier. "Actually, I had a relationship with a man for about three months a little over a year ago.''

''Was he a doctor?''

''Yes, he was a cardiologist at the hospital.''

''So, what happened?''

''I found out he was great at fixing hearts, but he didn't have one himself.'' His name had been Ben, and for the first time in her life she'd dropped all of her defenses. She snuggled deeper beneath the covers and continued. ''I thought everything was going fine. We saw each other when we were both free, which wasn't often, but we both understood the time constraints of our jobs. Anyway, it ended when I found out he was dating a nurse at the same time he was dating me.''

''Hmm, bad boy.''

She pulled one of the pillows to her chest, remembering the ugly scene that had ensued. ''When I broke up with him, he wasn't particularly nice about it,'' she confessed.

''Why? What did he do?''

''It wasn't so much what he did, rather it was the things he said.'' She heard the sound of Kevin shifting positions.

''Like what?''

She had never talked about it to anyone before, and she didn't know whether it was because she trusted Kevin so implicitly or because the darkness that surrounded them cast a kind of strange anonymity that was nonthreatening.

"He told me he'd only been dating me because he felt sorry for me, that I wasn't really his type because I didn't have a sexy bone in my body." The words tumbled out of her and the minute they left her mouth, she was mortified.

"You must have been hurt," he said, his voice a soft, silky caress.

"For a while, but then I realized he was just a jerk and I got over it. And now I guess we'd better get some sleep." Still embarrassed by her confession, she murmured a good-night.

"Good night, Phoebe," he replied and they both fell silent.

She was almost asleep when he called her name. "Yes?" she replied.

"If that doctor didn't think you had a sexy bone in his body, then he wasn't just a jerk, he was just plain stupid."

A sweet rush of warmth spread through her. "Thank you, Kevin."

"Just calling it like I see it," he said. And those were the last words they spoke that night.

Chapter Six

Kevin awoke only minutes before the alarm was set to go off. Being as quiet as possible, he reached over and shut the alarm off before it could ring. It was obvious from the utter silence of the room that Phoebe was still sleeping.

She was getting to him. With her bewitching green eyes and sweet lips, she had definitely gotten to him with her story about the doctor she had dated.

He couldn't imagine any red-blooded man not finding her incredibly sexy. What a jerk. Kevin found so much about her sexy…from the way she tucked her hair behind her perfectly shaped ear, to the way she wrinkled her forehead when she was deep in thought.

He looked over in the direction of her bed, wishing there were just a bit of light in the room so he could see her as she slept.

He had caught a glimpse of her the night before as she'd come out of the shower and before she'd escaped his view by crawling beneath the blankets.

She'd been a vision in pink, displaying a tantalizing length of shapely leg, the memory of which had kept him awake half the night.

Yes, she was getting to him and he didn't like it. He didn't like it one little bit. Silent as a shadow, he slid out of the bed, grabbed his gun from the nightstand then his clothes from the chair where he'd laid them the night before. He went into the bathroom, not turning on the light until the door was firmly shut.

For a long moment he stared at his reflection in the mirror, his gaze captured by the ugly scar that ripped down his chest. At the time of his life-saving surgery, he'd been given the option of having a plastic surgeon, but he hadn't been interested.

He realized now he'd wanted the ugly scar as a reminder that he wasn't the man his father had wanted him to be. It reminded him that he was a failure.

With a deep scowl creasing his forehead, he pulled on his T-shirt, then stepped into his jeans and strapped his gun at his ankle. He raked a hand through his hair, brushed his teeth, then stepped into his shoes, ready to begin another day in the car.

He left the bathroom and slipped over to the nightstand, where he clicked on the light to awaken Phoebe. The light apparently didn't penetrate her deep sleep as she remained unmoving.

He stood next to her bed, drinking his fill of her. Even without her green eyes flashing and dancing, she was lovely. Her features were delicate. Fine blond eyebrows, a small nose, and those sweet lips that were slightly parted as if awaiting a lover's kiss.

And it irritated him how much he wanted to be the lover that kissed her awake. He knew the taste of her lips, knew the heat of her kiss.

''Phoebe, wake up,'' he said, his voice more gruff than he'd intended.

She stirred slowly, stretching like a sleepy kitten, wincing slightly as she opened her eyes. Desire hit Kevin square in the gut, a burst of heat through his groin so intense he felt as if he was about to burst into an inferno of flames.

He backed away from her bed, needing to distance himself before he crawled beneath the covers with her and showed her just how wonderfully sexy he found her.

''We need to hit the road,'' he said, his voice sounding strange and unnatural to his own ears.

''And good morning to you, too.'' She sat up, her hair a tousled blond cloud, a sleepy cast to her eyes.

''Good morning,'' he replied tersely. ''While you get dressed, I'm going to load my suitcase in the car.'' Without waiting for her reply, he picked up his suitcase, unlocked the door and walked out into the predawn.

He drew a deep breath of the crisp, clean air, willing the flames inside him to subside. He checked his wristwatch, eager to get on the road. The faster he got her to California and Loucan, the faster he would be rid of her.

He waited only about ten minutes, then the motel room door opened and she joined him, her suitcase in her hand. He took her suitcase from her, trying not to touch her hand, trying not to smell the scent of her, a scent that had now become far too familiar.

''Let's get going,'' he said as he slammed the trunk closed.

He slid in behind the steering wheel as she got settled in the passenger seat.

''Are you always this surly when you wake up early?'' she asked.

''Always,'' he replied as he started the engine. ''And you would do well to remember that. I'm a surly, snoring slob.'' He wanted to be mad. Mad at himself for wanting her and mad at her for making him want her. But the ridiculous sentence that had just fallen from his own mouth diffused more than a little of his anger.

''Are you only surly, snoring and a slob on Saturdays or does it extend to other days of the week?''

He shot her a quick look and saw her eyes sparkling with a teasing light. Wasn't this rich? Somehow in the past twenty-four hours she had become more relaxed, more of an extrovert, and he was getting as uptight as a schoolmarm who'd accidentally wandered into a biker leather bar.

He drew a deep breath and released it slowly, consciously willing some of the tension out of his body. "The surly, snoring slob is sorry," he finally said.

"Apology accepted."

"Do you mind if I turn on the radio?" he asked after a moment of silence.

"Not at all. I like music."

He turned it on and tuned it to an oldies' station. As the car filled with the sounds of the Beach Boys, Kevin felt himself beginning to relax.

The surge of desire that had struck him so hard shouldn't have surprised him. It had been a very long time since he'd made love to a woman. He was a healthy, normal male and shouldn't be surprised that he was sexually attracted to a pretty woman like Phoebe.

In any case, it was difficult to remain surly with Beach Boys and Beatles songs filling the air. The sun was shining, all remnants of yesterday's rain gone.

They drove a couple of hours, then he pulled into a full-service gas station that offered strong coffee and flavored cappuccino. He filled up the tank, they got coffee, then hit the road again.

"Do you want me to take a turn at driving?" she asked.

He looked at her in surprise. "I thought maybe you didn't know how."

It was her turn to look at him in surprise. "Why would you think that?"

"You walk to work, you walk to eat. I figured you didn't have a car and probably didn't know how to drive."

"Actually, I have a car, a red Mustang Cobra. I keep it garaged not far from my apartment building. It's too much of a hassle to use it most of the time, but occasionally when I get a day off I like to crank up the radio and take a drive in the country."

"Whew, those are sweet little cars."

"I love it," she replied. "Anyway, do you want me to take over?"

"Right now I'm fine driving," he said. "If I get tired later I'll let you know."

As they had done the day before, at lunchtime they drove through a hamburger place and ate in the car. Occasionally he had to retune the radio station as they lost the signal of one and picked up new stations.

They both sang when they knew the words to the songs and he was grateful that she could more than carry a tune. There would be nothing worse than miles and miles of travel with a radio and a tone-deaf singer.

The miles clipped off beneath the hum of their tires against the pavement and Kevin found himself growing more and more relaxed. He'd always enjoyed driving and this long-distance trek was no different.

He cast a glance at Phoebe, who seemed to be as

relaxed as he was. Clad in a pair of jeans and a light-blue T-shirt, she stared out the window as if finding the landscape fascinating.

"Tell me about your time as a foster kid," he said.

She turned to look at him. "What do you want to know?"

He shrugged. "Over the years I've heard lots of horror stories about foster care."

"I don't have any real horror stories to tell," she replied. "For the most part, my foster families were all fairly decent people."

"Foster families?" he asked.

She nodded, her hair shining in the afternoon sunlight that streaked in through the windows. "That was probably one of the worst parts about being a foster kid. I'd just get used to a family and start to feel relatively settled in, then something would happen and I'd get shifted to a new family."

"You said one of the worst parts...what was another worst part?" he asked, genuinely curious about her past experiences.

She was silent for a long moment. "Probably the absolutely worst part for me of being a foster child was knowing that there was no unconditional love where I was concerned."

"I don't understand," he replied.

A frown creased her forehead and she crossed her arms in front of her, as if finding the air in the car a bit too cold. "It's hard to explain, but the most difficult thing for me to realize as a child was that nobody would ever love me with the kind of unconditional love that real parents offer their children. I always knew that the love my foster parents offered me was conditional. If I was good, and quiet and no trouble, they liked me, but if I wasn't all of those things, I was out of there.''

Kevin touched his chest as his thoughts turned to his own father. ''You know, sometimes real parents' love is conditional. So, how many families did you have in all?'' he hurriedly added, not wanting to delve into his own personal demons.

''I had a total of ten foster families from the time I was about two until I was sixteen.''

''Ten? That seems like an awful lot,'' he replied.

''Keep in mind I was very sickly when I was young, and that made it difficult to place me for any length of time. Nobody likes to deal with a child who is in and out of the hospital all the time.''

There was a wistfulness in her tone, as if she'd yearned for a real family, people who could offer her unconditional love, people who would love her and take care of her whether she was sickly or not, whether she was noisy or naughty or not. And for just a minute Kevin wished he could fulfill that need inside her.

He tightened his grip on the steering wheel and they once again fell silent. Day turned into evening and with each mile that passed, with every mile that brought them closer to California, Kevin found himself with mixed emotions where Phoebe and Loucan were concerned.

His job was to deliver her to the wharf in Santa Barbara where she could meet Loucan. That was supposed to be the end of his job.

Was he delivering her into more harm? Despite his best investigative efforts, he'd been unable to find out anything about the man who had hired him.

He knew Phoebe was desperate to connect with anyone who might know anything about her family, about her roots. What she didn't know was that if Kevin didn't like the lay of the land, if he sensed anything amiss, he would get her out of there faster than a lightning strike.

Phoebe was grateful when they stopped for dinner that night, once again opting to get out of the car and dine in so they could stretch travel-sore muscles.

It was just after six and the restaurant was packed with other travelers. They chose a booth next to a family who had a little girl who looked to be about two in a high chair at the end of the booth.

Almost immediately Phoebe was captivated by the pretty little girl who grinned and chattered as if she'd never met a stranger she didn't like.

The little girl also seemed completely enchanted by Kevin. She batted her long eyelashes at him and cooed, then offered him a bite of her mashed potatoes.

"Looks like you slay them starting at a very early age," Phoebe said to him teasingly.

He grinned and winked at the little girl. "She's just showing herself to be a woman of good taste already. At that age women are easy to please. Give them a lollipop and they love you forever."

"Ah, that sounds like a real cynic," she replied.

At that moment their waitress arrived to take their orders. While they waited for their food, Kevin made funny faces, making the little girl squeal and giggle with delight.

As Phoebe watched him, her heart expanded and she filled with an enveloping warmth. He would make a wonderful father, and if they had a little girl, she would look a lot like the one who was flirting and giggling with him at that very moment.

Phoebe hadn't thought much about having children until she'd begun dating Doctor Ben. At that time she'd experienced the awakening of maternal instincts she didn't know she possessed.

The hunger for a family, for children of her own hadn't left her when Ben had, rather the desire had increased. But, Kevin wasn't the man to give her those things, she reminded herself. He was on a mission to deliver her safe and sound to California and nothing more.

The family with the little girl left as the waitress was serving Phoebe and Kevin their food. "Have you ever thought about getting married and having a family of your own, Kevin?'' she asked once the waitress had departed from their booth.

''Sure, I think about it occasionally.'' He cut his steak, then looked at her once again. ''But I never think about it real seriously.''

''Why not?''

''I don't know, I guess I figure it's easier not to fail if you don't even try.''

She looked at him in confusion. ''What are you worried about failing at, being a husband or being a father?''

''I don't know, like I said, I don't ever think about it real seriously.'' He popped a bite of steak into his mouth, then asked, ''What about you?''

She knew it was a diversion. He was attempting to turn the topic of conversation from himself to her. She looked down at her soup bowl, then back at him. ''I don't know, I'd like to get married and have a family, but it's kind of hard when you don't even date.''

''I'll tell you one thing, if I were to get married and have children, I would definitely want more than one child.''

''Why?''

''As an only child I can attest to the fact that it's tough to have your parents' hopes and dreams all pinned on you alone.''

''Do you feel as if you let down your parents?'' she asked, aware that she was treading on dangerous ground, but wanting to know why his eyes darkened occasionally with shadows and why the mention of his father seemed to fill him with an unhealthy tension.

"Not my mom." He smiled, one of his quicksilver, slightly crooked grins. "She thought the sun rose and set on me."

"That's nice," Phoebe replied, a burst of envy sweeping through her. She wondered what it must be like to be so completely assured of another's love. "And your father?"

Kevin carefully cut off another piece of his steak, his gaze focused down on his plate. When he looked back at her she saw the darkened hue of his eyes, like storm clouds that needed to weep rain.

"I didn't know it until I quit the police department, but apparently my father's love was more conditional than my mother's. He couldn't believe that I wanted to do something different, that I was turning my back on the force. When I told him I was moving to California, he went ballistic, told me he was disowning me and had lost all respect for me."

She wished she could reach out and touch him, but something in his eyes forbade the gesture. "I'm sorry, Kevin, that must have been very painful for you," she finally said.

"It was rough," he agreed. "But, the real pain came from his dying before we got a chance to finally heal the breach between us. He was stubborn, and I guess I'm more like him than I realized. So, we didn't really get a chance to say goodbye to each other."

"So, his death was sudden?"

The darkness in his eyes seemed to lift a bit. "Yeah. He went home after work on night, got into bed and never woke up. He had a massive coronary." Kevin shook his head. "I always thought he was invulnerable. He was bigger than life...and certainly stronger than death, or so I thought."

"Regrets are painful to live with," she said.

"I don't regret quitting the force," he hurriedly replied. "What I do regret is allowing the distance to grow between my father and myself. It taught me that if you have something to say to somebody, you shouldn't let any grass grow on top of your tongue."

She couldn't help but smile at the image his words produced. He caught her grin and grinned himself. "You catch my drift?"

She laughed aloud. "I do." However, she didn't understand why his problems with his father would make him think he would be a failure as a husband and father. She would have liked to delve deeper, but was afraid she had dug deep enough.

They finished their meal, then returned to the car, deciding they could drive another couple of hours before finally stopping for the night.

This time she felt no real apprehension when she thought of the night to come. They had survived the small confines of a motel room just fine and she had slept like a baby. She assumed the arrangement would be the same tonight.

Her assumption was wrong she realized two hours later as she stepped into the room they had rented for the night. A king-size bed greeted them. She set her suitcase on the floor next to the door and looked at him in panic.

"The rooms with double beds were all taken," he said. "Look, if this is really a problem for you then I can sleep in the car."

She only had to look at him to realize that if she forced him to sleep in the car she would be one callous, selfish woman. He looked exhausted. "Don't be ridiculous," she replied airily. "We're both adults. I'm sure we can stay on our own sides of the bed."

"Once I hit the mattress, you don't have to worry about me moving a muscle," he said. He sank down on the foot of the bed and waved a hand toward the bathroom. "You get first dibs on the shower," he said tiredly.

"All right." She picked up her suitcase and headed for the small bathroom. "I'll hurry," she said, then disappeared inside.

She did hurry. She showered in record time and quickly pulled on her nightshirt. She packed everything else back into her suitcase, then carried it into the room where Kevin was sprawled, eyes closed, on top of the bedspread.

"I suppose you want me to move," he said, not opening his eyes.

"Just enough so I can slide under the covers," she said.

"All right, if you insist." He rolled off the bed and headed to the bathroom.

Phoebe quickly folded down the bedspread, this one a nauseating chartreuse, then she slid between the sheets.

She tried to make herself as small as possible, facing the wall and hanging on to the edge, leaving as much bed as possible for Kevin. Even so, as she imagined him lying next to her, the space they would share appeared far too small.

What she needed to do was fall asleep now…this instant, while he was in the shower. Then she wouldn't be conscious to experience the intimacy of sharing a bed with Kevin.

She closed her eyes, willing her breathing to slow, willing her muscles to relax. But no part of her body was listening to her, everything was tense, as if expecting something to happen.

She grew even more tense when the sound of the shower running stopped and a few moments later he came back into the room.

"If you get any closer to the edge, you're going to fall off the bed," he said.

Drawing a deep breath she turned over to look at him, surprised to find herself slightly disappointed to see that he was clad in a clean white T-shirt and a pair of jogging shorts.

"I just didn't want to crowd you at all," she replied.

He grinned. "I can handle a little crowding better than I can handle you waking me up by bouncing off the floor." He got into the bed and patted the space between them. "See, plenty of room without crowding each other." He reached over and flipped off the light. "Good night, Phoebe."

"Good night, Kevin," she replied.

But he was wrong. He was crowding her with his very presence so near to her, with his freshly showered scent surrounding her and with his body heat radiating out to warm her.

He was crowding her with his charming smiles and sexy eyes that occasionally darkened with pain. She could tell the exact moment when he fell asleep. His breathing grew deeper, more regular and a tiny snore emitted from him. Rather than bothering her, the snore seemed endearing and that worried her. That worried her a lot.

Knowing he was sound asleep, her body finally relaxed and, matching her breathing to his, she also fell asleep.

Lightning rent the sky, thunder exploding like a cannon overhead. She was in the ocean, fighting waves the size of skyscrapers, fear so thick in her throat she was afraid she would suffocate.

The sea was a bubbling caldron, the sky a torment of sound and fierce flames of electricity. Terror ripped through her, but something else was inside her as well…a deep well of mourning that was sheer agony. But she didn't know for what she mourned…didn't know why her heart felt as if it were ripping in two.

Somehow she knew if she remained in the sea she would die, and if she left the sea she would die as well. She cried out, wanting somebody…anybody to save her…to take her from the sea, to take away her anguish.

"Phoebe."

The voice came from far away…a familiar voice amid the crashing of thunder and sizzle of lightning. "Help me," she cried, but she wasn't sure she had spoken aloud.

"Phoebe, honey, you're having a bad dream."

Kevin's voice. With the recognition of that voice, the sea vanished. The thunder muted. The lightning disappeared. She was in the bed lying next to Kevin…right next to Kevin.

"Shh, it's all right. You're safe here." His voice was deeper than usual. She could tell he was half asleep even though his hand stroked her hair.

"Come here." His hand reached out and pulled her closer against his side. "Come on, now. Go back to sleep, I won't let anything happen to you."

She hesitated only a moment, then placed her head on his chest. His warmth surrounded her and his hand continued to caress her hair. ''Shh,'' he hissed. And fell back to sleep.

His shirt smelled of fresh laundry detergent and she could hear the sound of his heartbeat beneath her ear. She closed her eyes. She had never felt more safe in her life.

It was at that moment that she recognized what was happening in her heart. She was falling in love with Kevin Cartwright.

Chapter Seven

She awoke with the room still in darkness, Kevin's chest still her pillow beneath her head. One of his arms was around her back, as if to hold her in place against him and their legs had become entwined in their sleep.

She didn't move. Kevin still slept soundly, his body a warm heat against hers, his breathing deep and even. She knew she should move away, but she remained perfectly still, relishing the feel of his muscled chest beneath her cheek, the beat of his heart in her ear and the feel of his solid body against hers.

For just this moment she wanted to wallow in the emotion that had claimed her last night before she'd fallen asleep after her nightmare. She'd fallen asleep with love for Kevin in her heart, in her soul.

She breathed in the scent of him, trying to capture it in her lungs, sear it into her memory for the time when he would leave her and go back to his own life.

She had to admit, she was vaguely disappointed that he'd seemed so unaffected by their sleeping arrangement. She almost wished he'd tried to take advantage of her. At least she would have known then that he found her physically appealing.

The buzz of the alarm clock made her jump. He slapped a hand at the clock, silencing the buzzer at the same time he tightened his grip around her back to keep her in place.

"What a great way to wake up in the morning." His sleep-husky voice sliced through the darkness of the room. "A cheap motel room and a gorgeous woman in my arms. This could almost make me happy to be awake so damned early."

Despite the pressure of his arm around her, Phoebe reluctantly rolled away from him. "Kevin, I'm sorry about last night," she said, finding it easy to apologize to him with the room still plunged in darkness.

"Sorry about what?"

"About waking you up with my nightmare."

"Don't apologize," his voice was soft...gentle. "I've got a few night demons of my own that occasionally bother my sleep."

"You have nightmares?" she asked.

He was quiet for a long moment. "Just one. Over and over again."

"What is it? What do you dream about?" she asked curiously.

"What is this? I'll show you mine, if you show me yours?" He turned on the lights and the intimacy of the darkness was shattered. "How about we get on the road. We've got about five hours of driving and we'll be in Santa Barbara."

As he dressed in the bathroom, Phoebe tried to sort out the myriad emotions that soared through her. The night of sleeping in his arms had made her feel unusually vulnerable.

When he left to take his suitcase out to the car and she dressed, she tried to tell herself it wasn't love she felt for him. She'd just been grateful to have somebody pull her from the landscape of her nightmare, somebody to hold her close and keep the terror, that awful sense of loss, at bay.

He was already seated behind the steering wheel when she exited the room and walked out into the dawn light of a new day.

Today they would be in Santa Barbara. Today she would be able to smell her nightmare, taste the brine on her skin, see the waves that so terrified her in her dreams.

She might also get the information that she had yearned for all of her life...information about a family she'd never known.

They started the day with fresh coffee from a

nearby coffee shop, then headed for the interstate and the last leg of their journey.

As she sipped her coffee, she found herself shooting gazes at Kevin, aware that her time with him was drawing to an end. They hadn't spoken about what would happen once she was introduced to Loucan, but she assumed Kevin would go back to his life in Los Angeles and she'd take a flight back to Kansas City. End of story.

"So, tell me about the nightmare you had last night," he said.

"First you tell me about yours," she countered.

"I can't." He gazed at her, then back at the road. "I always know I've had it when I wake up, and I always know it's a familiar nightmare, but I never remember any of the particulars."

Phoebe wrapped her arms around herself to ward off a sudden chill. "I wish I didn't remember the particulars of mine."

"It sounded pretty bad. You were moaning and crying and thrashing about."

Despite the chill that seeped through her bones, her cheeks warmed with embarrassment. "I've had the dream for as long as I can remember. There's a storm...a terrible storm with lightning and thunder. Wind roars like a freight train and the rain slashes my skin and I'm in the ocean."

"You mean on a boat or a raft or something?"

She shook her head and frowned thoughtfully. "I

don't know. I have no concept of how I'm in the ocean, just that I am."

Again he looked at her, his eyes as blue as the sky outside the car window. "And it's the storm that scares you?"

"Yes, but it's more than that." She hesitated again, unsure how to explain what it was she experienced each time she had the nightmare.

"I feel like I'm going to die, that if I leave the sea I'll die, yet if I stay in the sea I'll die. And my heart isn't just filled with fear, but with an ache that makes it feel as if it's breaking apart." She gave a little unsteady laugh. "Crazy, huh?"

"You know, there are people who analyze dreams and say that the dream is never about what you see, but is filled with symbolism. You know, like maybe the ocean symbolizes life and you're frozen, afraid to live yours to the fullest."

She eyed him dubiously. "Do you really believe that?"

"Nah. For the most part I think dreams are just plain weird and don't have much meaning at all."

"I agree, but this one bothers me because I have had it for as long as I can remember and it's always the same."

His blue eyes darted to her once again. "Did any of your foster families ever take you out in a boat? Is it possible you're reliving some memory?"

"I don't remember ever being in a boat, and I certainly don't think I've ever been in the ocean.'' The very thought sent a new chill coursing through her. ''I did have one family that liked to spend time at the beach, but I never went near the water.''

''So, you don't know how to swim?''

''No. Although when I see people swimming, it looks relatively easy.''

''It is relatively easy,'' he replied. ''Maybe if we have some spare time I can teach you how to swim.'' He smiled sympathetically. ''Don't get all tense. We don't have to swim in the ocean. We can start in the motel pool.''

''I don't know. Maybe,'' she replied vaguely, although with the memory of her nightmare still fresh in her mind, she didn't want to think about getting anywhere near a body of water.

She turned her attention out the window, watching the passing landscape without any real interest. Had she been in a boat sometime in the first two years of her life? Was what she dreamed not a nightmare, but some sort of repressed memory?

She inwardly scoffed at the very idea. Why would a two-year-old be in a boat during a storm? It didn't make any sense. Just like somebody trying to steal her necklace made no sense.

''We should be in Santa Barbara by lunchtime,'' Kevin said, breaking into her thoughts.

''Have you contacted Loucan to tell him we'll be arriving then?''

"No. I'll call him when we arrive." His forehead wrinkled in a frown. "Phoebe, I know how eager you are to talk to Loucan, to find out what he might know about your family. But I'm telling you here and now, if I don't like the way things are going, if I sense that you're in danger of any kind, we're out of there."

Phoebe nodded, too moved to speak. Apparently his interest in her wasn't just a matter of the fee he would get upon delivering her to Loucan, but something more than monetary gain. That only made her feelings for him more confusing.

She smelled the ocean long before she saw it, and the familiar scent filled her with a new tension. She sat up straighter in her seat as they entered the outskirts of Santa Barbara.

"Have you been to Santa Barbara before?" Kevin asked, slowing his speed to adhere to a lower speed limit.

"Once, when I was about eight. My foster family at the time came to visit and sightsee here."

"You never told me exactly what part of California you lived in," he said.

"Santa Monica, Long Beach, mostly Southern California towns."

"I'm going to check us in at a motel near the wharf where I always meet with Loucan. There's a nicer hotel nearby, but if anyone is looking for us I imagine that's the first place they'll look."

"Do you think somebody is still looking for us?" she asked worriedly.

He hesitated a moment and she saw his fingers tighten slightly on the steering wheel. "Kevin, didn't you promise me the truth and nothing but the truth?"

"All right, the truth," he finally said. "I've been thinking a lot about the men who tried to get that necklace from you and their relationship to Loucan."

"And what have you come up with?" she asked.

He slowed, then stopped at a red traffic light. Looking at her, his expression was somber. "If these men aren't working for Loucan, which I don't believe they are, then it's fair to guess that they're working against Loucan."

She nodded her agreement. "That makes sense to me."

"Then, what I believe is that they don't want you to make contact with Loucan and that means we are most vulnerable right now. I have a feeling they are going to do everything in their power to keep you and Loucan from connecting."

A horn blared behind them, letting them know the traffic light had changed from red to green. Kevin turned his attention back to the road while Phoebe contemplated what danger might yet await them.

The motel room was just as tacky as Kevin remembered it from the last time he'd seen Loucan. The only thing in its favor was a double door that led out to a small balcony with a perfect view of the ocean.

In deference to Phoebe and her nightmare, he walked around the two double beds and to the window where he began to draw the curtains closed.

"You can leave it open," she said, although her features were strained. "I'm aware of the fact that a view of the ocean can't hurt me. I just don't want to go near the water."

He sat in the chair by the desk, gazing at her intently. "You know the place where we meet Loucan is right on the water."

She nodded, the movement a terse jerk of her head. "I know."

He had an intimate knowledge of fear and his heart went out to her. "I'll hold your hand if it will make you feel better," he said with a gentle teasing tone.

Those beautiful green eyes of hers held his gaze with a kind of intense desperation. "Actually, it would make me feel better," she replied softly.

Something in those eyes of hers, some emotion he couldn't quite discern, made him break eye contact with her. "Why don't you get settled in and relax a little. I'm going to try to contact Loucan and scout out the area."

He stood and grabbed his cell phone from the pouch on the side of his suitcase. "Dead-bolt the door after me and don't worry, I'll be just outside."

She followed him to the door and he had the craziest impulse to kiss her goodbye before leaving the room. Instead, he raked the back of his hand down her cheek. "And try to smile," he said. "I promise you everything is going to be fine."

She grabbed his hand and held it to her cheek. "I'm going to hold you to that promise," she said, then released his hand.

He heard the dead bolt being shot into place immediately after he stepped out. He drew a deep breath, hoping he could make good on the promise he'd just made to her.

Leaning against the bumper of the rental car, he punched in the numbers that connected him to the mysterious Loucan. As usual, there was no answer on the other end of the line, but merely a beep to indicate that a message should be left.

"We're here in Santa Barbara," Kevin said, then broke the connection. He knew from past experience that Loucan would get back to him, although he wasn't sure when. There were times Loucan returned his call within minutes, other times when it was a day or two before he heard back from the man.

In the meantime, Kevin was going to share a motel room with a woman who was making it more and more difficult for him to ignore his intense physical attraction to her.

Waking up this morning with her in his arms had filled him with a longing he'd never before experienced, the longing to wake up every morning to the same perfume filling his senses, the same slender curves warm against him.

He rubbed his chest, the scar of his shame evident beneath his shirt. Phoebe was a beautiful, desirable woman who deserved far better than him.

Still, he wasn't about to leave her hanging here in California until he knew exactly what Loucan wanted from her and exactly why her necklace was so important.

He returned to the room, knocking so that Phoebe could open the door for him.

"Did you get hold of Loucan?" she asked.

"Not yet." He pulled his cell phone charger from his bag and plugged it into an outlet. "I left a message and told him we were here in Santa Barbara. He'll call when he gets the message."

"So, what do we do until then?" she asked.

He stretched out on the bed he had claimed as his own. "Wait." He picked up the remote control for the television and clicked it on. "Try to relax, Doc."

"Easy for you to say," she replied dryly, but she lay down on her bed and propped the pillows behind her head.

Within minutes, she was asleep.

Watching her sleep was far more interesting than watching the sitcom rerun on the television. She looked even softer in sleep, more vulnerable, and he knew he'd seen more of this side of her than any of her colleagues.

He knew that with him she'd let down her guard, allowed him closer than anyone else except maybe the stupid doctor without a heart that she'd dated. And he felt a responsibility for her as he'd never felt for another human being in his life.

He closed his eyes, not wanting to look at her anymore. He awakened a little over an hour later, hunger pangs drawing him from his sleep.

He opened his eyes and saw Phoebe looking out the window. Although her back was to him, he could see the tension that filled her. "Facing your demons?" he asked.

She turned to look at him, her eyes momentarily haunted. "Something like that," she replied, then turned back to the window. "It's funny, I'm deathly afraid of the water, and yet somehow seem drawn to it at the same time."

"I'll tell you what I'm drawn to," he said as he sat up and raked a hand through his hair. "I'm drawn to the idea of dinner. What about you?"

"I am hungry," she agreed and turned away from the window. "Just let me freshen up a bit."

As she disappeared into the bathroom, Kevin looked at his watch. It was just a few minutes before five. It would be good for both of them to get out of the confines of the motel room for a while. The less time he spent in this room with Phoebe, the better.

Minutes later they were back in the car, seeking a

restaurant that looked interesting, yet had no view of the ocean.

"Do you like Mexican?" he asked as he saw a flashing sign for The Cantina just ahead.

"Love it," she replied.

He wheeled into the restaurant parking lot, glad to see the lot starting to fill despite the relatively early hour. It was a testimony to either cheap drinks or great food. He hoped it was the latter.

They were seated almost immediately in a semi-dark booth with a candle glowing in the center of the table. Spanish music played from a sound system, the volume low enough to encourage conversation.

They both opened the oversized menus and studied the fare. Kevin tried to ignore how the candlelight caressed the strands of her hair, making the soft strands appear almost silvery. When she'd freshened up, she'd put on a touch of blush and a mauve lipstick that emphasized the lushness of her lips...lips now pursed in a tantalizing moue as she studied the menu.

"What are you having?" she asked, her green eyes leaving her menu to meet his.

"The Rancho Special. Beef enchilada, beef and bean burrito, an oversized taco and rice. What about you?"

"Certainly not that," she exclaimed. "That's way too much food for me. I think I'll have a chicken enchilada." She closed her menu and pulled her napkin onto her lap.

"How about a margarita?" He gestured to a waitress who walked by, a couple of margaritas on her tray.

"Oh, I don't think so," she demurred. "Alcohol always makes me sleepy."

"That's not necessarily a bad thing," he replied. "We're just going to go back to the room and go to bed anyway."

"But what if Loucan calls?" she asked. "I want to be completely clearheaded when I meet him."

"He won't call tonight," Kevin said, going on past experience with the man. "If I haven't heard back from him now, it will be morning before he calls."

"Maybe a margarita will relax me a bit," she hedged.

"I agree." What he was hoping was that she'd have a drink, get drowsy and go right to sleep once they got back in the room. What he didn't want was any after dark, intimate conversations to draw him any closer to her.

A waitress appeared at the table and he placed their order. "You aren't having a drink?" Phoebe asked when the waitress departed.

"Nah, one of us has to remain clearheaded," he said teasingly. "Besides, I'm driving."

Moments later he realized that ordering her a drink had been a bad idea. He held his breath, watching as she licked the salt from the rim of the glass, then took a sip.

"Are you sure you don't want to change your mind and order one of these?" she asked. "It's wonderful." Again her dainty pink tongue swirled at the salt and Kevin felt his blood pressure soar to dangerous levels.

"No, thanks, I'm fine." He looked around the restaurant, seeking anything that would keep his attention away from Phoebe. He wasn't fine.

He was fevered with want, fighting an overwhelming desire to hold Phoebe in his arms, ravish her lips and caress the silky strands of her hair, the creamy texture of her skin.

Would it be so terrible to make love to her if he made certain she understood that he was making no promises, intended no future?

"Kevin?"

Her soft voice pulled him from his heated thoughts. "What?"

She looked down at her drink, then back at him, her eyes shining with an earnest light. "I just wanted to tell you thank-you for all you've done for me."

He smiled humorlessly. "I've disrupted your perfectly normal life, led bad guys to you who ransacked your house and attacked you. I've brought you to the place of your nightmares and who knows what awaits us tomorrow. Why on earth are you thanking me?"

She reached across the table and took his hand in hers. Her fingers were cool from the drink, but quickly warmed with the contact with his. "Thank you for making me feel safe despite the danger that's lurked around the corners.'' She squeezed his fingers, then released his hand. ''Thank you for being such a nice guy.''

''You're welcome,'' he said and released a deep, long sigh. She'd effectively banished his thoughts of making love to her without any promises or a commitment.

Although he'd love to make love to her, how could he possibly do it knowing the only future he intended to share with her was a separate one?

Chapter Eight

The alley smelled of spoiled garbage and dark, ugly secrets. Kevin advanced slowly, cautiously, his gaze focused on the woman slumped between two overflowing metal garbage cans.

Her legs were sprawled out, her worn leather skirt hiked up high enough that he could see her bright red panties.

But it wasn't her panties that drew his attention, it was her blouse. Once white, the front of the lacy blouse had a bright-red blossom of blood in the center.

Kevin knew he should wait for backup, but if he waited too long, she would be dead. She moaned, a faint, low whisper. Kevin's breathing filled his own ears, harsh and rapid.

Where was the perp? He'd had no opportunity to get out of the blind alley. Kevin had been driving by the entrance of the alley when he'd heard the hysterical scream of the woman as she'd been stabbed.

He'd screeched his patrol car to a halt and jumped out, his gaze never leaving the alley between the Chinese restaurant and the X-rated video store.

This was the armpit of Chicago, a rough neighborhood of criminals that was part of Kevin's beat. Gunshots and screams here were as normal as the sounds of lawnmowers and crickets in the suburbs in springtime.

Where was the perp? Kevin gripped his gun with both hands, pointing it first to the left, then to the right as he advanced.

He recognized her as he drew closer. She was a regular, a crack-addicted prostitute named Honey who he'd arrested at least half a dozen times. If Kevin was to guess, her pimp was the one responsible for her current condition.

Sweltering heat surrounded him as he deliberately made his way toward her. Her moans were fainter now and he could see the glistening of the blood that seeped from a wound in her upper chest.

"Help is on its way," he said to her. Before the words had completely left his mouth, he caught a blur of motion in his peripheral vision.

John Joseph Casey, aka JJ, crashed his huge body into Kevin, dislodging his gun from his hand. As the gun skittered out of reach into the garbage near a tin can, JJ's fist slammed into Kevin's jaw.

Kevin was a cop, a good cop with well-honed physical skills, but he didn't have a chance against the ex-con who had the build of a large mountain and the temperament of an enraged pit bull.

Knowing in a fistfight he was at a decided size disadvantage, Kevin attempted to talk to JJ. But as the man pulled out a large fillet knife, his eyes glittering with the wildness of a crazed, caged animal, Kevin decided to forgo any attempt at verbally bonding with the man.

He started to back away, his gaze never leaving the knife that glittered wickedly in the faint light from a nearby street lamp.

Sweat trickled down his back, along the sides of his face. JJ was known to like his drugs, and by the look in his eyes, Kevin recognized the man was high on something.

He heard the sound of a siren in the distance, but the siren seemed to transform JJ from a dangerous man into a dangerous monster.

JJ lunged at Kevin and the two men tumbled to the ground. Pain, a pain Kevin had never experienced before seared through his chest. Couldn't breathe. He...couldn't...breathe....

Kevin jerked awake, gasping for breath, his body covered with a fine sheen of perspiration. The room was in darkness and he sat up in an attempt to control his ragged breathing.

The dream. No, it wasn't a dream, but rather the reliving of a nightmare. Five years ago Kevin had been in that alley. Five years ago Kevin had nearly died in that alley.

He was grateful that he apparently hadn't awakened Phoebe, but knew from experience it would take some time before he could go back to sleep once again.

What he needed was fresh air. He needed to draw deep breaths and let the night air cool his fevered skin. As quietly as possible he slid from the bed, then just as quietly unlocked and opened the door that led out onto their small balcony.

He closed the door behind him and walked to the railing. The moon was full overhead, spilling down a luminous glow that was oddly comforting in the aftermath of his night demons. He yanked off his damp T-shirt, allowing the salty cool air to play over him.

He laid the shirt across the back of one of the two chairs so the air could dry the remnants of his dream, then returned to the railing, drawing deep breaths of the salt-scented air.

If he'd needed a reminder of all the reasons why he shouldn't get involved with Phoebe, or anybody else for that matter, he'd just had one. The nightmare had been a vivid, visceral memento of Kevin's failure, first as a cop, then as a man.

The waves spilling to the shore made a rhythmic sound that was calming, and after drawing a few more breaths, he sank down in the chair opposite of where his shirt was drying.

It had been nearly eight when they'd returned to the room after dinner. They'd showered and gotten into their respective beds, then turned on the television to pass a little time before going to sleep.

She'd confessed that she rarely had time to watch television and he'd turned the channel to a popular sitcom, enjoying the sound of her laughter as she seemed to lose herself in the silliness.

He wondered what it would be like to be snuggled up next to her on an overstuffed sofa, a bowl of popcorn within easy reach and her in his arms?

What would it be like to spend each evening watching television with her, then going to sleep in each other's arms? What would it be like to drink his coffee each morning with her across the table from him?

The memory of her in his arms the night before caused every muscle to tighten up inside him and it hadn't taken long before he realized the confines of the motel room were too small, too intimate.

All he had been able to think of was the short little nightshirt she wore and the white cotton bikini briefs she probably had on beneath it.

Sleep had been a relief, easing the desire that had simmered within him for the past two days, a desire he feared would only serve to hurt her if allowed to be released.

And he didn't want to hurt her. He had a feeling she'd suffered a lifetime of hurt, fighting feelings of abandonment, keeping herself distant from others so as not to be hurt anymore.

He hoped she got the kinds of answers she needed from Loucan, answers that would make her whole. He hoped she left here with a sense of identity, a peace that would help her to reach out to others and eventually find the kind of love she richly deserved.

He leaned his head back and closed his eyes, wondering why on earth the idea of Phoebe finding love with somebody else filled him with such sadness.

He awakened to dawn creeping across the sky and Phoebe stepping out of the door onto the balcony. He jumped out of his chair and grabbed for his T-shirt, but he knew it was too late. She stared at his scar and he braced himself for her revulsion.

"I see I'm not the first surgeon in your life," she said and took a step closer to him.

"Yeah, it's pretty gross, isn't it?" He fought the impulse to cross his arms over the old wound, try to shield it from her eyes.

"Gross?" Her gaze flew to his. "More like interesting." She reached out and touched the puckered skin. "Punctured lung?" she asked.

"Yeah," he replied, feeling the same sort of

breathlessness as when his lung had been depleted of air.

Her fingers were so warm against his skin, and clad only in the pink nightgown, her hair in slight disarray from her sleep, she looked achingly beautiful.

Her finger moved lower, following the ridge of his scar. ''Spleenectomy?''

He nodded, unable to speak. ''It's not gross, Kevin,'' she chided him. ''It's just skin that has a boo-boo.'' His breath caught in his chest as she leaned forward and pressed her lips to his scar.

The desire that had been simmering just beneath the surface for so long exploded into sweet flames of fire.

He grabbed her hand and pulled her to him, crashing his lips to hers as his arms wound around her and pulled her tightly against him.

She leaned into him, eagerly opening her mouth to his, further enflaming him as her arms reached up around his neck. Her mouth was hot, her body cool from the breeze coming off the water.

With just the thin cotton of her nightshirt between them, he could feel the thrust of her breasts against his chest and he wanted to remove the nightshirt, allow their bodies the intimate touch of lovers.

When he finally broke the kiss, she took his hand and pulled him back into the privacy of the room. Her eyes glowed with green fire and her lips beckoned him to enjoy another kiss.

He couldn't deny the invitation and with a small groan, he kissed her once again. He wondered vaguely if he kissed her long enough, deep enough, if it would be enough to staunch the hunger inside him. Somehow he didn't think so. One kiss, no matter how long, no matter how deep, would never be enough.

They fell onto her bed, mouths clinging, hands clutching. Even though in the back of his mind a tiny voice whispered that he should stop this before it went too far, but he didn't want to stop…not now… not yet.

She lay on her back and he was atop her, his arms wrapped around her back. Their mouths drank of each other's while her hands caressed his back, tangled into his hair.

His reticence to begin something that he didn't intend to finish was being drowned beneath the sensual pleasure of her warm mouth, her shapely curves and the overwhelming emotions that rose up inside him.

He tore his lips from her mouth and instead kissed the smooth, creamy skin of her throat. She moaned, a tiny little sound that only served to enflame him further.

His hands moved from behind her to caress down her sides…down to her waist, then back up again where he cupped her breasts through the material of her nightshirt. Her nipples were hard, pressing against the cotton as if begging to be freed.

She pushed him off her and sat up. With her gaze locked with his, she pulled the nightshirt over her head, leaving her clad only in a pair of white bikini panties and the silver necklace whose charm winked from between her naked breasts.

Kevin had a single moment of lucidity, a moment where he knew the best thing for both of them was to call a halt to any further kissing, any more caressing. Then, she opened her arms to beckon him back to her, and he was lost.

The questions that had flurried through Phoebe when she'd first seen Kevin's scar had vanished for the moment, lost beneath a greater need. Never in her life had she wanted to be held, to be kissed, to be loved by anyone as much as she wanted that from Kevin.

As she returned to his arms, his mouth once again seeking hers, she felt an absolute rightness resound in her heart. It was as if she'd waited a lifetime for this man, for this moment.

It didn't matter to her that she'd known him such a brief time. She felt as if she'd known him for an entire lifetime. He was the man her heart had sought and tears of joy pressed at her eyes as his lips razed down her throat.

His hands were sweet warmth as they caressed her breasts, his thumbs raking over her nipples, sending electric tingles shuddering through her.

She knew he was aroused and she felt sexy and desirous as she never had before. Nothing she had experienced with Ben had prepared her for the magnitude of feelings and sensations that now swept through her.

She was aroused not only physically, but mentally...emotionally. All the hunger she'd ever known seemed sated in Kevin's arms and tears of joy burned at her eyes as she felt the kind of connection with another that she'd always longed to have.

"Kevin, make love to me," she whispered, wanting to complete what they had only just begun. She wanted...needed him to take complete and sole possession of her.

She knew instantly that her words had the opposite effect on him that she had wanted. He stiffened against her, then sat up.

His eyes were a deep, midnight blue, filled with desire, tempered with regret. He drew a deep breath as if to steady himself and raked a hand roughly through his hair.

"We have to stop," he said, his voice slightly unsteady. "We have to stop before we do something we'll both regret."

She placed a hand on his arm. "If we made love, I wouldn't regret it."

He shook off her touch and got up from the bed. "Trust me, you would regret it." He walked over to the chair and grabbed his jeans and pulled them on.

Phoebe, shivering slightly, reached to the foot of the bed and picked up her nightshirt and drew it over her head. Disappointment swelled thick in the back of her throat, disappointment mingling with more than a little bit of hurt.

Had she misread what she thought had been his desire? Had he not been responding to her as intensely as she'd been responding to him?

His gaze held hers for a long moment and she felt as if he was reading her mind, reaching into her very soul. "Don't get me wrong, Phoebe, there is absolutely nothing more I'd like to do at the moment than make love to you. I've been fighting a bad case of wanting you from the moment I first laid eyes on you."

She scooted to the side of the bed, but remained sitting, looking at him in confusion. "Then, I don't understand."

Again he raked a hand through his brown hair, a deep frown furrowing his forehead. "I'm not looking for any kind of a relationship," he said. "You're a nice woman and you deserve a good man."

She was more confused than ever. "And you aren't a good man?"

His eyes as he held her gaze were suddenly haunted. "No, I'm not."

Of course she knew better. In a million ways in the last week he'd shown himself to be a man of honor, a man of compassion...a good man. But she could also tell from the yawning darkness in his eyes that he'd closed up on her as effectively as a clam.

He grabbed a clean shirt from his suitcase, then his cell phone. "Why don't you get dressed and we'll go out and get some breakfast."

She desperately wanted to talk to him, to find out what mysteries hid inside him. She sensed a scarring far more profound than the one that marked his chest, but any further conversation was impossible as he left the room while yanking on his shirt.

As she dressed, she tried to ignore the fact that her body still tingled with the imprint of his caresses, her lips still burned from the intensity of his kisses. No matter what he said to her, she believed he cared for her...didn't he?

She had to be more than a job to him. She had to be more than a payoff. But she knew she was rather naive when it came to the relationships between men and women, knew that it was possible she was reading Kevin all wrong.

What she wasn't reading wrong was her own feelings where he was concerned. What she felt for him wasn't mere gratitude, it wasn't lust, it wasn't friendship.

It was love.

With Ben she recognized now she had kept a large part of herself guarded, that she hadn't allowed her heart to get involved, too afraid of being hurt.

With Kevin her heart was already involved and she

had no defenses. She had a mysterious man named Loucan dangling the promise of a family and the aching dream that what she felt for Kevin would be reciprocated. But her greatest fear was that she would come away from California without any knowledge of her family and even worse, once she met with Loucan, Kevin would be out of her life for good.

They drove in an uncomfortable silence to a nearby restaurant. Dawn had transformed into day, the sky a cloudless blue overhead.

The restaurant offered both indoor dining and outdoor, oceanview tables. Phoebe was grateful he chose to sit inside, obviously thoughtful enough to know that the sight of the water would unsettle her.

They ordered their meals and were served cups of coffee, then the waitress departed their table. Phoebe wrapped her fingers around the warmth of the coffee mug, looking at Kevin, who seemed to be avoiding her gaze.

"How did it happen?" she asked.

"It happened in an alley five years ago when I was a cop," he said, not trying to pretend he didn't know what she was asking about. "A woman had been stabbed in the back of a blind alley and I responded without backup. The perpetrator was high on drugs and mad as hell. He managed to get me down, then tried to gut me like a fish."

"From the looks of your scar, he nearly succeeded,'' she replied, horrified by what he had gone through.

''Yeah.'' He reached up a hand and touched his chest, his eyes once again haunted. ''He damn near managed to kill me.'' He folded his fingers around his mug and stared down into the liquid. ''I was already unconscious from blood loss when backup arrived. He managed to slice up two other cops before they took him down.''

''Did they kill him?'' she asked.

He shook his head. ''He's serving a life sentence behind bars.''

''And it was after that when you quit the force?''

''Yeah.'' He looked up at her, a touch of irritation evident on his features. ''Look, can we talk about something else? That happened a long time ago and has nothing to do with here and now.''

Phoebe wanted to protest, but at that moment the waitress appeared with their orders. They ate in the same uncomfortable silence that they'd driven to the restaurant in, and Phoebe desperately wished she knew how to breach the distance that yawned between them.

It was especially painful to recognize that the physical intimacy they had shared seemed to have created his emotional distance from her now.

She could abide the silence no more by the time they finished the meal and were lingering over coffee.

"Kevin," she began softly, aware of other diners around them. "Please don't shut off from me."

"I'm not," he said quickly. "I've just been thinking."

"About that night? Is that what your nightmares are of?"

Again his hand moved to his chest and she realized it was an unconscious gesture she'd seen him often do. "Yeah, I occasionally have a nightmare about that night." He picked up his butter knife and ran his thumb over the edge. "I'll tell you one thing, I've definitely gained a healthy respect for sharp instruments."

He was trying to joke, but the darkness in his eyes belied the forced lightness of his voice. Words of love rose to Phoebe's lips. More than anything she wanted to tell Kevin of the love that filled her heart for him. But at that moment his cell phone rang.

He answered, listened for a moment, then said okay and hung up. "That was Loucan. We're to meet him in fifteen minutes."

Apprehension rose up inside Phoebe as she realized she was about to meet the man who just might have the answers to the questions that had plagued her all of her life.

Was this the beginning of a life of connection to family for her? Would she finally find out what had happened to her parents? If she really had siblings?

Strange, that she'd waited for this moment her entire life, yet what really filled her with anguish was wondering if this was the end of any relationship with Kevin.

Chapter Nine

"The official name of this beach is Arroyo Burro Beach, but the locals call it Hendry's Beach," Kevin explained as he pulled into a parking lot at the public beach.

He shut off the car engine and looked at Phoebe. One look at her and he realized she probably hadn't heard a word he'd said. She stared straight ahead, as if transfixed by the sight of the ocean waves breaking to the shore. Her fingers were curled into her palms, her knuckles white.

The most difficult thing he'd ever done in his life had been to stop their spontaneous lovemaking earlier that morning and gain some necessary distance from her.

Now he found that distance difficult to maintain as he saw her obvious anxiousness.

"Phoebe?" he said softly. When she didn't respond, he called her name again louder.

She turned to him, a flush to her cheeks. "I'm sorry, what did you say?"

He pointed to the restaurant in the distance where there were a dozen or so tables on a pier. "That's the Crab's Claw where I always meet Loucan. He is always seated at the table nearest the water." Her face blanched of color and despite all his intentions to the contrary, he reached out for her hand.

Her hand clung to his in a kind of desperation. "I know it sounds ridiculous, but suddenly I'm scared," she said.

"I told you it's going to be fine," he said with an assurance he didn't feel. This whole thing suddenly felt bad and he wasn't sure why. "Phoebe, just stay close to me and if I tell you it's time to go, don't ask questions, don't hesitate, just come with me."

She squeezed his hand even harder and nodded. "I'm ready." She released his hand and drew a deep breath. Her eyes lost some of their fear. "Oh, Kevin, I hope he can tell me something about my family. I hope this isn't all just a horrible mistake."

"I hope not, too," he replied softly.

Together they got out of the car and headed down the path that led to the restaurant's main entrance. "Too bad it didn't take Loucan a day or two to get in touch with us," he said as they walked side-by-side.

"Why?" she asked.

"Don't you remember? I was going to teach you how to swim. A little breaststroke, maybe some freestyle." He did swimming motions with his arms and was rewarded by her smile.

"You're being silly to try to relax me."

"Is it working? Because if it isn't I've still got the butterfly and the backstroke to show you."

"Kevin, I've lived twenty-seven years without knowing how to swim." She stopped walking for a moment and turned to face him. "Trust me, I'm not planning on jumping into the ocean anytime soon."

He looked at her for a long moment, memorizing how she looked at this very moment. The morning sun caressed her features, giving her skin a warm glow and sparking in her hair.

She wore a green pastel short-sleeved dress. Although slightly wrinkled from being packed, it complimented the color of her eyes and displayed her slender curves to perfection.

Her eyes had lost some of their fear and had begun to sparkle with anticipation. This is how he wanted to remember her, looking so beautiful her vision ached in his chest.

"Come on, Loucan should be waiting for us."

The Crab's Claw was typical of many of the oceanside restaurants that dotted the shoreline. With plank floors and fishing nets decorating the walls, it was obvious the place catered to tourists and offered casual dining.

They walked through the main dining room toward the door in the back that led out to the outside tables. Through the windows that lined the wall of the dining room, Kevin could see Loucan seated at one of the tables.

Although Loucan faced away from them, there was no way to mistake his powerful build, the dark brown hair and the deep, rich tan the man sported.

He seemed to sense their presence as they stepped out of the door, for he stood and turned to face them. As always, Kevin was struck by the man's well-defined, strong features.

He stiffened slightly as he saw Loucan's piercing blue eyes drift slowly down the length of Phoebe in a gaze that was decidedly nonfamilial.

"Ah, Kevin," he said, directing his gaze to him when they reached where he stood by the table. "Good to see you again. And you," he took Phoebe's hand in his, "you must be Phoebe."

"Yes," she replied.

"Please, let's sit. We have much to discuss," Loucan said as he released Phoebe's hand.

They sat at the table, Loucan between Kevin and Phoebe. "You are more beautiful than I dreamed," Loucan said to Phoebe and again Kevin noticed the man seemed to be looking at Phoebe as a delicious morsel of food rather than a long-lost family member.

"Thank you," Phoebe replied, her cheeks coloring a pretty pink.

"We've come a long way for some answers, Loucan," Kevin said, hoping he didn't sound as surly as he felt.

Loucan nodded, his gaze still on Phoebe. "You have the piece of metal?"

Phoebe hesitated a moment, looking at Kevin for reassurance. He nodded and she pulled the necklace from the neck of her dress. She leaned toward Loucan and he took the charm in his hand and eyed it closely.

"It is what I've sought," he said softly. "You are one of four who I have sought."

"Who am I?" The question fell softly from Phoebe's trembling lips.

Loucan released the charm and leaned back in his chair. "In order to tell you who you are, I must first tell you a story you will find difficult to believe." He paused as a waitress appeared at their table.

They ordered coffee, and once the waitress left, Loucan looked at Kevin. "Was there any further trouble on your way here?"

"No. We took every precaution we could to make certain we weren't followed." Kevin shot a glance around the area. "Of course, that doesn't mean that nobody knows we're here now." He looked back at Loucan. "And I hope you're going to explain exactly who is after Phoebe and her necklace."

Loucan nodded. "As soon as we get our coffee, I

will tell you all that I know.'' He looked back at Phoebe. ''I understand you're a surgeon.''

''Yes, although I must confess that my work and my life seem very distant at the moment. I'm anxious to hear what you can tell me about my family.''

Loucan reached out and touched her hand once again and Kevin felt his ire rising. ''A little patience, then I'll tell you everything I know.''

Kevin was grateful when the waitress arrived with their coffee, then left once again. He wanted Loucan to tell Phoebe what she wanted to know, then he wanted to get her out of here. He didn't like the way Loucan looked at Phoebe, the way he touched her. Kevin sure as hell hadn't brought Phoebe all this way to be seduced by the mysterious Loucan.

Once again Loucan leaned back in his chair, his gaze going to the ocean behind Phoebe. ''I assume you are both familiar with the legend of Atlantis,'' he began.

Kevin frowned, wondering what on earth the legend of some sunken civilization could possibly have to do with Phoebe.

''Bear with me,'' Loucan said, as if reading Kevin's thoughts. ''The legend of Atlantis, in part, is true. There was an island in the middle of the Pacific, an island of advanced culture and science, that was sunk when a volcano erupted. But it wasn't Atlantis, it was Pacifica.''

"What on earth does this have to do with Phoebe?" Kevin asked impatiently.

Loucan held Phoebe's gaze intently. "Because Pacifica is the place of Phoebe's birth."

Kevin stifled his impulse to snort his disbelief at the utter nonsense of Loucan's words. "I don't understand," Phoebe said. "If the island sank, then how could I be from there?"

"The volcanic action formed a dome of earth over the island and trapped air in a pocket that protected the people of Pacifica. Over the years the people of Pacifica adapted with the help of science and nature, allowing them to be at home both on the land and in the sea."

Kevin frowned, unsure exactly what he meant. He looked at Phoebe to see how she was swallowing this tale. To his surprise there was nothing on her features but interest.

Loucan took a sip of his coffee, then continued. "Over the years two factions arose in Pacifica. Phoebe, your father was King Okeana and he ruled Pacifica for many years. He believed that the people of Pacifica were best served by staying isolated from the rest of the world. His faction was the Swimmers."

The man was a lunatic, Kevin thought. Baying-at-the-moon delusional. He started to stand, deciding they'd heard enough, his heart heavy as he realized he'd led Phoebe on a wild-goose chase.

"Kevin, please," she said softly, as if knowing his thoughts. "I want to hear all of it."

He settled back in his seat with a sigh of resignation. If she wanted to listen to this mumbo jumbo, he wasn't going to be the one to stop her. He picked up his coffee cup and indicated that Loucan should continue.

"The other faction, known as the Breathers, were led by a man named Galen, my father. When you were just a toddler, Phoebe, war broke out between these two factions. Your mother, Queen Wailele, was one of the first casualties, and after her death, your father appointed a guardian for each of his four children and sent them out of Pacifica. The guardians were told to protect the children, raise them with the memory of Pacifica and return in fifteen years."

"Trealla," Phoebe said softly.

Loucan nodded. "She was your guardian. Your father had no way of knowing she would die when you were nothing more than a baby and you'd be denied all knowledge of the land where you belong."

"And the necklace?" Phoebe asked.

"Before your father sent his four children away, he locked away in an underwater cave some of the scientific treasures of our land. He sealed it and broke the seal into four pieces, one to go with each of his children.

"Seven years ago the war finally ended with the death of your father and four years ago my father sent me out to hire a detective and try to find the four of you.''

He leaned forward and took one of Phoebe's hands in his. "I will be completely honest with you, Phoebe. We need your part of the seal and are hoping we can find your sisters and brother to get their pieces of the seal as well. But, as important, we need you back in Pacifica to help the healing process from the war begin. If you, as a daughter of King Okeana, and I, as the new king of Pacifica, can show a united front, it will go a long way in beginning to heal the wounds that this war has left behind.''

The sight of Phoebe's dainty hand nearly swallowed in Loucan's larger one unsettled Kevin. He breathed a sight of relief as she pulled her hand from his, a frown of concentration marring her lovely forehead.

''You said earlier that the people of Pacifica adapted to their environment with the help of science and nature,'' she said. ''I'm a woman of science, Loucan, a doctor. What exactly do you mean? How did they adapt?''

''Over the years, the people became able to swim in the ocean with membranes that changed their legs into tails and produced gills to allow them to breathe underwater.''

''That's it,'' Kevin said and stood. ''I'm not going to sit here and let you try to tell Phoebe that her family is...is...a school of fish.''

"Mers, Kevin, not fish," Loucan replied with a touch of frost to his voice.

Kevin stared at the man in disbelief. "So, you're telling me Phoebe is a mermaid?"

"Exactly," Loucan replied.

Kevin looked at Phoebe. Her features seemed to be set in stone. "Come on, Doc. I think we've heard enough."

She stood and Loucan rose as well and placed a hand on her arm. "Phoebe, Pacifica needs you and we need your necklace. I know that the information I've given you sounds fantastic and unbelievable, but please consider what I've told you." He dropped his hand from her arm, his gaze intense as it lingered on her. "I'll be back here all evening if you want to talk some more."

Phoebe nodded, although Kevin was certain this would be the last time they'd see Loucan. He and Phoebe walked back through the restaurant the way they had come, neither of them speaking.

Kevin felt bad. He didn't look at her as they walked to the car. He knew the vast disappointment that must be weighing heavily in her heart.

He'd brought her here in hopes of finding something out about her family and instead she'd listened to the delusional rantings of a madman.

Phoebe tried to tell herself that Loucan was crazy, that the stories he'd told about a place called Pacifica were patently unbelievable, but there was no doubt that the handsome, powerful man who called himself Loucan had believed what he'd told them. His belief had radiated from his eyes, unwavering and intense. But of course, that didn't mean that she believed them.

As they walked toward where the car was parked, Kevin threw an arm around Phoebe's shoulder. "Phoebe, I'm so sorry." His voice was thick with his regret.

She looked at him in surprise. "Why are you sorry?"

"Because I was hoping you'd get some real information about your family, not some crazy legend twisted by a nut."

"You didn't know what he was going to tell me," she replied.

They reached the car, and to her disappointment, he dropped his arm from around her and leaned against the passenger door. "No, I had no idea what he was going to tell you and I still can't believe what I heard. Maybe I couldn't find any background on him because he's spent his life in a mental institution."

"Maybe," Phoebe replied, thinking again of all that Loucan had said.

Kevin moved aside and opened the door for her and she slid into the car. Moments later, they were on the way back to their motel room.

"I guess we can get a good night's sleep and start

back to Kansas City in the morning,'' Kevin said as he turned into the motel parking lot.

''There's really no point in you driving me all the way back to Missouri only to have to come back to California. I can get a flight back.'' The words caused a ball of intense sorrow to swell in the back of her throat.

She would get on a plane and leave and would probably never see Kevin Cartwright again. It was just as she'd imagined, she was leaving with no information about her family and only her love for Kevin burning in her heart.

''I'm not sure I want you on a plane by yourself,'' he said as they entered their room. ''We still don't know who is after you or why you're in danger.''

Phoebe drew her necklace from her dress and clung to the charm, her thoughts playing and replaying Loucan's words. ''We should have asked Loucan.''

''Yeah right, he would have probably told us a band of werewolves are after you,'' he said dryly.

Phoebe rubbed her forehead and opened the door that led to the small balcony. She stepped outside into the salty air, leaned against the railing and stared out at the expanse of ocean.

Even though her logical mind rebuked everything that Loucan had told her, she couldn't absolutely and irrevocably dismiss his words.

Something inside her, something that had nothing

to do with logic or rationale refused to let go of the crazy possibility that Loucan was telling the truth.

She heard Kevin step out on the balcony behind her. "You all right?" he asked softly.

"I don't know," she said truthfully. "I'm confused."

He came to stand next to her, his shoulder warm against hers. "Phoebe, surely you don't believe any of the nonsense Loucan said about a land beneath the sea and people who can grow tails."

"No...yes..." She sighed in frustration. "I'm not sure what I believe." She turned to face him, noting that his eyes matched the cloudless sky overhead. "I keep thinking about my reoccurring nightmare, that maybe it isn't a dream at all, but rather a memory of when I was sent away from Pacifica. The grief I feel in the dream was probably because not only was I leaving behind my home, but I was also separated from my sisters and brother."

"Phoebe." He placed his hands on her shoulders and gazed intently into her eyes. "I know how badly you wanted to find out something about your family, but how can you possibly believe anything that Loucan told us?" He dropped his hands to his sides.

"I don't know," she said miserably. She turned her attention back to the water and frowned thoughtfully. "I only know there are some things that seem to coincide with what Loucan told us."

"Like what?" he asked incredulously.

"Like how I'm desperately afraid of the water, yet strongly drawn to it as well. Like the fact that according to Loucan this necklace is vitally important and somebody besides Loucan is trying to get it from me." She looked at him once again. "How do you explain that?"

He raked a hand through his hair. "I don't know," he confessed. "But I'm sure not willing to make the leap that somehow it's tied to a bunch of mermaids and mermen."

Phoebe looked at him for a long moment, then quickly turned back to face the ocean, tears blurring her vision. It was time to tell him goodbye. His duty to her was over. And that thought ached more deeply than the fact that she hadn't found any of the family members she'd never known.

She was suddenly overwhelmed with grief and she could no longer contain the tears that burned so harshly at her eyes, the sobs that pressed so thick in her throat. A sob escaped her lips and she pressed two fingers against her mouth to stop the next one, but it was no use.

"Ah, jeez, Phoebe. Don't cry." With a clumsiness that was endearing, he whirled her around and pulled her against his chest, his hand patting her back gently.

She hid her face in his shirt, which smelled of sunshine and his familiar scent, and smelling his fragrance only made her tears fall faster.

"I know you're disappointed, Phoebe, and I'm really sorry about all this."

"I'm not crying because of that," she said between sobs.

"Then why are you crying?"

The emotions she'd been fighting to keep inside her for the past two days suddenly refused to be contained any longer. She stepped out of his arms, for some reason angry that he didn't know what she felt, that he couldn't guess what was in her heart.

"I'm crying because our little adventure is over." She swiped impatiently at her tears. "I'm crying because tomorrow I'm probably going to get on a plane and return to my miserable, lonely life."

He took a step toward her, but she backed away, afraid she would shatter into a million pieces if he touched her in any way.

Again she wiped her tears from her eyes, wanting to look at him and see him clearly, without the blurring effect of her sorrow. "I'm crying because somehow I've managed to fall in love with you and I don't want to tell you goodbye."

She nearly laughed at his stunned expression. If it hadn't been so painful she might have. But the fact that he looked so utterly surprised simply caused her pain to increase.

"Phoebe..." He reached out a hand toward her, then quickly jabbed both hands into his jeans pockets. "You're upset, you aren't thinking clearly. Hell, just a few minutes ago you were trying to convince yourself that you're a mermaid.''

''I might not know where I come from or who my family is, but I know the emotions that are in my heart.'' She took a step toward him. ''I love you, Kevin. With all my heart, with all my soul, I love you.''

This time it was he who retreated from her. He stepped back, pulled a hand from his pocket and raked it through his hair. ''Stop saying that,'' he said, a touch of desperation in his voice. ''You can't love me. You don't even really know me.''

There was something in his eyes...something that gave her courage, that filled her with a shining ray of hope. ''But I do know you,'' she said softly. She took another step closer to him, emboldened by the fact that he didn't step away.

She placed a palm on his cheek, gazing at him intently. ''I know that you like to tease to break tension, that your sense of humor is secondary only to your sense of compassion. I know that despite your irreverence about your job and life in general, you feel things deeply. I know that I love you, and that's really all I need to know about you.''

His eyes blazed with anger and he grabbed her wrist and tore her palm from his face. ''You don't know me at all.'' He stepped away from her, his mouth a thin slash, his features twisted with emotion. ''Don't love me, Phoebe. Trust me, I'm not worth the effort and there won't be a happily-ever-after here for you."

Although his final words cut through her with a stab of agony, she shoved her own pain aside as she tried to understand the anguish that rode his handsome features.

"What are you talking about, Kevin? What makes you think you aren't worth the effort?"

"Because I'm a coward, because I quit the police department because I was scared." The words exploded out of him in a tone of intense suffering. "I let down my fellow cops and I lost my father's respect, my own self-respect. Trust me, Phoebe. You don't want to get involved with me. I'm not worth the trouble." With these final words he turned and disappeared into the room, leaving Phoebe alone on the balcony.

Chapter Ten

Kevin sank down on the foot of his bed, depleted from his outburst and still reeling from Phoebe's words of love. There had been just a moment, when she'd said she loved him, that his heart had leapt with joy and dreams of marriage and white-picket fences had sprung full-blown to his mind.

But that moment had been fleeting, crushed beneath the weight of reality. He was a loser, and nothing was ever going to make him good enough for a woman like Phoebe.

He looked up as she came in from the balcony, her eyes slightly reddened from her tears, her features somber. She sat on the foot of her bed and gazed at him. "Tell me about that night in the alley," she said.

He sighed wearily. "I already have."

"You didn't tell me everything. You didn't tell me about your fear and you didn't tell me why you think you're nothing but a coward."

The last thing Kevin wanted to do was to go back to that time in his life, but somehow he felt as if he owed it to her to explain. He couldn't tell her he loved her, because he refused to allow himself that emotion, but he could tell her what had brought him to the emotional state that denied her his love.

"I already told you what happened in the alley, that I was stabbed. Loss of blood made me pass out before the perp was apprehended and I was rushed to the hospital. But in those minutes, or seconds before I passed out, I felt the worse fear that I'd ever felt in my life."

"Kevin, you'd just been stabbed by a drug-crazed maniac. You should have felt fear."

He dismissed her words with a shake of his head, a sickness filling his stomach as he remembered the crippling fear that had lingered in him like a dreadful disease. "The moment I got through surgery and knew I was going to live, I also knew I wasn't man enough to go back to being a cop."

Unable to look at her, he stared at the television screen directly in front of him as he relived those days and weeks, months and now years of shame. "I was too afraid to go back to chasing criminals and upholding the law. I was scared to death that I'd be a liability to the force and my fellow officers. I was also scared that at some time I might have to face another man with another knife and that next time I wouldn't be so lucky...or worse, I'd run and leave another officer in jeopardy.''

''And so you intend to punish yourself for the rest of your life?'' She rose from her bed and to his dismay sat next to him. Instantly her floral perfume filled his senses. ''Kevin, you had a horrible, near-death experience and you reacted like a normal human being.'' She reached out a hand to cover his, her eyes beseeching him. ''Isn't it time you stop beating up on yourself?''

He yanked his hand from hers and stood with his back to her, needing to distance himself from her. Why was she making this so difficult? Why couldn't she see that she deserved a whole man, not one who still suffered nightmares and was scarred by his own cowardice.

''You've fallen in love with me, haven't you, Kevin?''

Her voice was a mere whisper coming from behind him. He closed his eyes and drew a deep breath in an attempt to control the thick emotion that pressed tight against his chest.

He had consciously kept himself from examining his feelings for Phoebe, had known deep inside that he did love her. And while he desperately wanted to deny his love for her not only to her, but to himself, the words wouldn't come.

Turning to face her, he fought for control. "It doesn't matter what I feel for you," he said, injecting all the dispassion he could into his voice. "All that matters is what I intend to do about it and I intend to do nothing. Tomorrow, I either take you back to your life in Kansas City or I put you on a plane to return to your life. In either case, there is no future for you with me."

Her eyes were filled with a bleak despair and tears sparked there, tears Kevin felt in his very soul. But he knew he was doing the right thing and refused to be swayed from his position of isolation.

"That drug addict in that alley, he intended to kill you?" she asked.

Kevin's hand shot to his chest, where the scar marred not only his skin, but his soul. "Yeah, I'd say that was his intent."

Tears trekked down her cheeks as she continued to hold his gaze. "He succeeded, didn't he? Because a man who can't give love, a man who refuses to accept love is dead." She got up from his bed and once again disappeared out the door leading to the balcony.

Kevin watched her go, a hollowness resounding inside him. He'd lived with a certain amount of emptiness inside him since that night so long ago, when fear had driven him off the job he loved, away from the people he loved and respected.

But this ache seemed deeper, more profound and he knew it had to do with the fact that despite all his intentions to the contrary, he'd somehow managed to fall in love with Dr. Phoebe Jones.

He wished it were tomorrow, that he was either driving her back home or putting her on a plane. He wanted the goodbyes over and done with.

Stretching out on his bed, he wondered how long she would remain outside and if she was still crying. He wanted to go out and console her, to dry her tears, but he knew that was the worst thing he could do. He needed to keep his distance until they parted ways. He didn't want, in any way, to give her hope that things could somehow, would somehow be different.

She remained outside until midafternoon, then came inside and curled up on her bed with her back to Kevin. He remained on his back, staring at the ceiling and wondering how long this whole episode would infect him with sorrow.

He awoke at dusk, his gaze immediately going to the bed next to his. He sat up as he realized Phoebe wasn't there. At that moment the door to the bathroom opened and she stepped out.

He sat up as he realized she'd changed clothes. She was now clad in a white blouse and skirt and had her purse in her hand. "What are you doing?" he asked.

"I want to go speak with Loucan again."

"Why?" He hoped his rejection of her hadn't somehow made her more desperate to believe the outlandish tales Loucan had spun.

"Kevin, Loucan hired you to find a woman named

Phoebe who had this necklace. I don't know where the truth lies, but that much can't be denied. And that means maybe he can tell me more about my sisters and brother and why somebody else is after this necklace.''

''I don't think Loucan knows the difference between truth and fiction,'' he replied.

''I need to talk to him again, Kevin. I can't go home without knowing for certain that Loucan is truly a dead end.''

He nodded and stood. ''Just give me a minute or two to freshen up myself.''

Minutes later they were once again in the car headed for Hendry's Beach. The sky was painted in pinks and oranges as the sun slowly inched its way beyond the horizon.

''Do you think he'll be there?'' she asked as he pulled into a parking space.

He shrugged. ''He said he would be here this evening. That means eventually he'll show up. If he isn't there when we arrive, we can order some dinner while we wait.'' He was grateful that she apparently didn't intend to discuss any further their personal relationship. They got out of the car.

''What happens if we walk this way?'' She pointed to a path that led along the shore.

''It follows the waterfront and eventually comes to a pier that leads to the outside dining at the restaurant.''

"Then let's go that way," she said.

Knowing her fear of the water, he eyed her dubiously. "Are you sure?"

She hesitated a moment, then raised her chin and nodded. The path led onto the sandy shoreline and silence once again fell between them as they walked toward the pier in the distance.

"You okay?" he asked after a minute or two.

She flashed him a determined smile that pierced through to his heart. "I'm fine."

"When we reach the pier just don't lean against the railing. I've noticed before that it's pretty rotten." He looked ahead and spied the table where the three of them had sat only that morning. "It doesn't look like Loucan is there yet."

"Then I guess we'll order dinner," she replied.

They came to the wooden walkway that led up from the water and toward the pier and the restaurant. They had nearly reached the pier when a clattering of footsteps behind them made them both whirl around.

Phoebe gasped at the sight of a dark-haired man rushing toward her. "It's him," she cried. "He tried to get my necklace."

The words barely got out of her mouth before Kevin yanked her behind him, now standing between her and the man on the narrow walkway.

"Give me the necklace and nobody will get hurt," the man snarled. Before Kevin could reach down for his gun, there was a tiny snap and a switchblade with a wicked length of blade appeared in the man's hand.

The dying sunlight glinted on the blade and Kevin's blood turned frigid. The scar on his chest throbbed with a visceral memory of pain and his heartbeat banged in his ears.

An ugly smile curved the man's lips. "Before you can get to that gun on your ankle, I'll make you into shark bait then fillet her."

The threat to Phoebe sent shock waves of rage through Kevin, vanquishing any fear that might have been inside him. With a roar, he charged the man, his gaze never leaving the shank of the knife.

He couldn't allow this man near Phoebe. There was no way he'd allow him to hurt her and the only way he could be sure of that was to gain control of the knife.

He dodged the initial jab and managed to grab the man's wrist. As they grappled, their bodies slammed from one side of the walkway to the other and the sound of crackling wood rent the air.

Kevin was vaguely aware of Phoebe's cries as he struggled to both evade being cut or stabbed and get the knife from the attacker. As he held the man's knife hand with one hand, he grabbed his long dark hair with the other and attempted to slam his head against the railing.

As their body momentum collided with the rotten railing, a loud snap resounded and suddenly the two men were airborne. Kevin held tight to the man's hand and hair, hoping...praying that the water beneath them was deep enough to absorb their spontaneous fall.

The last sound he heard before they hit the water was Phoebe's high-pitched scream. They plunged deep beneath the surface of the water, the blow of the impact springing their bodies apart.

As Kevin fought to get to the surface, he frantically tried to find his adversary. A sharp, stabbing pain in his back forced the air from his lungs and he whirled around to see the man behind him. Kicking at him, he gasped as he surfaced, dragging air into his starving lungs.

Instantly he looked left, looked right, watching, waiting, for the man to surface for air as well. But no head broke the water and as seconds passed, Kevin wondered if his kick had rendered the man unconscious.

Kevin looked up at where Phoebe stood, her face white. He gave her a wave to indicate he was all right, then began to swim toward the walkway where she stood. He reached up to grab a support beam beneath the walkway, intending to pull himself up and out of the water.

He pulled himself up and was about to climb out when something slammed into his back with a white-hot impact that instantly loosened his grip on the beam and expelled all breath from his body.

He slid back into the water, wondering how on earth the man had managed to stay underwater for so long and where he was now. Kevin knew his lung had been punctured, just as he knew he was probably going to drown. The water around him turned red and a killing lassitude overtook him.

Fighting to stay afloat, he looked up at Phoebe, all kinds of regrets sweeping through him. Then he slid beneath the surface of the water.

Phoebe watched in horror as Kevin's head disappeared from view. She'd seen the man stab him in the back, knew that Kevin was hurt. She glanced around frantically, wondering why her screams hadn't brought any help.

She looked back at the water, sobbing in relief as Kevin once again broke the surface. His face was white against the blue water…too white and she could see red in the water, indicating that he was bleeding. He went under again.

She knew if she stood there long enough she would watch him either die from his wounds or drown. Without immediate help he was going to die.

Drawing a deep breath, a chill racing up her spine, she knew the only thing she could do was brave the water that had haunted her for a lifetime. Without giving herself a chance to think of anything other than helping Kevin, she jumped in.

Impact with the cold water shocked her. Down.

Down. Down, she went, instantly panicked. She didn't know how to swim. In all probability she had just turned one tragedy into two.

As her body stopped its downward plunge, she moved her arms, opened her eyes and looked to find Kevin. She couldn't see him, but began moving upward. The initial panic she'd felt dissipated a bit as she felt the water embracing her and she was filled with a crazy sense of familiarity.

The only thing that disturbed her was a prickling sensation in her legs that grew more and more intense as she frantically searched the water for Kevin. She had no idea what had happened to the man who had attacked Kevin. She hoped...prayed he'd swam away, afraid that her screams had summoned help.

Lungs ready to burst, she surfaced just long enough to draw deep breaths, then plunged under once again, terrified that when she found him it would be too late.

She kicked her legs to move forward, intense pain ripping through them. What was happening? She felt something changing...transforming...a painful transformation that frightened her.

When she kicked her legs again, she realized she no longer had legs...an iridescent green tail had taken their place. She had no time to assess, no time to marvel at the fact that she was breathing beneath the water.

She had to find Kevin. With the powerful tail she now possessed, she cut through the water with speed, nearly sobbing in relief as she saw Kevin's legs up near the surface of the water. If he was that close to the surface, then he was breathing in air. And that meant he was still alive.

With a flip of her tail, she raced toward him, but before she could reach him, he slid down into the water once again. She swam to him, saw his eyes widen as she reached his side, then those blue eyes rolled back in his head and she knew he was unconscious.

She grabbed him, his weight light in the buoyancy of the water and she headed toward shore. As she hit shallow water, pain once again gripped the lower portion of her body and by the time she hit the shoreline, the tail was gone, replaced by her slender legs.

Pulling Kevin up on the sandy shore, she became aware of the sounds of people and looked up to see that a crowd had gathered on the restaurant pier.

"An ambulance is on the way," one of them called to her.

She nodded and turned her attention to Kevin. Thankfully he was breathing, but his breathing was labored. With an effort, she turned him on his side and checked the wound on his back.

It looked deep, but the cold water had helped to staunch the bleeding. Although he was unconscious, she was grateful that at least he was breathing.

Within minutes there were people around them and

the ambulance arrived and Phoebe climbed into the back to ride with Kevin to the hospital.

During the brief ride, she held his hand as an oxygen mask was placed over his nose and mouth and his vitals were checked. Her heart pounded frantically as she eyed his handsome, but pale white, features.

The moment they arrived at the hospital, Kevin was whisked away, leaving Phoebe to wait in the emergency waiting room.

She had never been in this position before—she'd always been the one inside the emergency room working frantically to save somebody's life. She sank down on one of the plastic chairs, her wet clothing chilling her in the air-conditioned room.

A nurse came by and brought her several towels, a blanket, and thong sandals and pointed her to a nearby rest room where she could dry off a bit.

Inside the rest room, she rubbed the towels over her skirt and blouse in an attempt to pull out most of the moisture. Spying an air hand dryer, she walked over to it and punched the button and stood in front of the warm air until the machine shut off.

She punched the button several more times, first facing the stream of warm air, then turning around so it could help dry the back of her.

When she felt sufficiently dry once again, she stepped up to the mirror and stared at her reflection. *You are a mermaid.* The words filled her head with stunned wonder. Everything Loucan had told them was true. He wasn't crazy. He wasn't delusional. As unbelievable as it seemed, she was a mermaid.

If Loucan had been telling the truth about that, then he must have been telling the truth about her family. Somewhere she had a brother and two sisters. The joy that winged through her was tempered with despair as she thought of Kevin.

Kevin, who had braved a knife to save her life. Frantic for news, she quickly left the rest room and returned to the waiting room.

She wanted to tell somebody that she was a surgeon, that whatever was wrong with him she would fix. She wanted to tell somebody to please make him okay because he was the man she loved with every ounce of her being.

Instead, she could do nothing but sit...and wait.

Kevin knew he was dreaming. He knew because he was beneath the sea and swimming with a mermaid. The mermaid had sparkling green eyes that matched her tail. Phoebe. God, she made a beautiful mermaid.

He smiled and reached for her and she came into his arms and with the water embracing them, they shared a sweet kiss of endless passion.

"I think he's coming around," an unfamiliar voice said.

Kevin frowned, wanting the voice out of his dream.

"Kevin?"

He smiled, recognizing the second voice. Phoebe.

"Kevin, can you open your eyes?"

Of course he could. He could do anything for her. After all, he loved her. He opened his eyes and it took a minute for him to orient himself.

He was in a hospital bed and Phoebe sat in a chair at his side. It all flooded back to him...the confrontation, the fight in the water, the white-hot pain that had stolen his breath.

"Kevin." She reached for his hand, her eyes brimming with tears.

"Are you all right?" he asked.

She laughed through her tears and squeezed his hand. "I'm fine and you're going to be fine, too."

"I'll just leave you two alone," a nurse said from nearby. She left the room and closed the door behind her.

"So, what happened?" Kevin asked.

"You were stabbed twice. One was superficial, the other punctured your lung, but thankfully did no other damage. Oh, Kevin, I was so afraid that you were going to die." Tears once again spilled down her cheeks.

"Come here, you." He motioned for her to lean forward and he took his thumb and gently swiped at her tears. "I guess it's going to take more than a couple of knives to be the end of me."

"You didn't even hesitate," she said, awe in her

voice. "Even though he had a knife, you charged him anyway."

"I was afraid he was going to hurt you," he replied thoughtfully. "It's funny," he continued. "I remember in that second when he pulled the knife that fear swept through me, but it wasn't the kind of paralyzing fear I'd always imagined I'd feel if confronted by danger again."

She leaned closer, her eyes shining with an emotion that couldn't be mistaken...it was love. "That's because you aren't a coward, Kevin."

"Ah, but I have been a coward," he replied. He held up a hand to still her protest. "I promised you the truth and nothing but the truth a couple of days ago, so now you're going to get it. I've been a coward because I've been afraid to admit how much I love you, because I've been scared that somehow I'd let you down."

Again tears poured down her cheeks. "Kevin, you could never...ever...let me down."

"The truth is, Phoebe, I can't stop thinking about how wonderful it would be to go to sleep each night with you in my dreams, to wake up every morning with you in my arms. I can't stop thinking about how great my life would be if you were in it all the time."

He struggled up to a sitting position, for the first time in five years feeling a true happiness and a rightness. "I know you have your work, your life in Kansas City. I'd be willing to move there if you'd marry me. Marry me, Phoebe.''

Joy radiated from her features, followed swiftly by a look of such utter misery it shot a new knifelike pain through him. ''I'd love to marry you, Kevin,'' she said, emotion thick in her throat. ''But I've got something to tell you that might change your mind.''

Her eyes threatened to spill tears once again, and in their sparkling depths Kevin remembered the vision he'd had under the water just before he'd passed out. He'd seen Phoebe swimming toward him, her hair floating around her face, her arms stroking and her green, iridescent tail undulating to move her through the water.

He stared at her in shocked surprise. He'd thought perhaps it had been a delusion, but he realized now it had been true. He drew a deep breath, knowing it was going to take some time to adjust to the reality he'd just learned about her. Did it matter to him? Not a chance.

''Phoebe, come here.'' He patted the bed next to him. She hesitated, but he reached out and grabbed her hand and pulled her down on the bed beside him. ''Come here, sweetheart and let me whisper in your ear.''

She looked at him curiously, but bent down closer to him. ''I can't believe I was trying to teach a mermaid to swim,'' he whispered.

She sat up, her gaze startled. ''You know?''

"I know. I still can't really believe it, but I know what I saw."

"It's true, Kevin. I can hardly believe it myself, but it's true."

He pulled her closer to him, gazing at her with all the love he had in his heart for her. "Phoebe, I promised you the truth, right?" She nodded, her lower lip trembling as if she was expecting the worse. "Okay, the truth is I don't care if you turn into a can of salmon every night at dusk, I love you."

He leaned forward and claimed her trembling lips with his own. She responded eagerly, wrapping her arms around his neck and pressing herself against the length of him.

Although his body ached from his wounds, he wasn't about to tell her so. He was willing to risk the discomfort for the utter wonder of kissing Phoebe.

"Does this mean you'll marry me?" he asked when the kiss finally ended.

Those shining eyes of hers told him the answer before her lips even moved. "Oh, yes, Kevin. Yes," she replied and again their lips met for a kiss that illuminated every dark corner of their hearts, filled every ounce of emptiness that might have resided there.

It was a kiss that promised love and passion, laughter and a life together forever and always.

Epilogue

"It looks as if the patient is going to live." Loucan hesitated just outside Kevin's hospital room where the midmorning sun shone bright into the windows.

Kevin was dressed and he and Phoebe were seated on the bed, awaiting the doctor's order of discharge. "I'm guess I'm a tough cuss," Kevin said and wrapped his arm around Phoebe's shoulder.

"May I come in?"

"Please," Phoebe said.

Loucan came into the room and sat in the chair facing the bed. "I heard what happened and wanted to make sure you were all right."

Phoebe grabbed Kevin's hand and smiled up at him as he assured Loucan that he was fine. She still couldn't believe the events of the past twenty-four hours, but one thing she absolutely, positively believed in was Kevin and his love for her.

"Loucan, I have so many questions for you," she said.

His piercing blue eyes looked from her to Kevin, then back again. "And I had a question for you, but I believe I have my answer."

"And what was that?" Kevin asked.

"I explained to you about the warring factions in Pacifica and how it is now my greatest hope to bring peace. The best way to have done that would have been for Phoebe and I to unite in marriage for the good of our land. But I see her heart is otherwise involved."

"And it's going to stay 'otherwise involved,'" Kevin replied tersely. "And I've got a question for you. Who was the man who tried to get the necklace from Phoebe? Who's the guy who stabbed me yesterday evening?"

Loucan frowned. "It had to be somebody who is working with Joran."

"Joran?" Phoebe asked.

"He's the leader of a group of rebels who are attempting to secure the pieces of the seal for their own gain."

"Loucan, tell me again about my family. Can you tell me anything more about my siblings?"

"Saegar, your brother is one of the cursed ones we call meremers."

Phoebe frowned. ‘‘Cursed how?’’

‘‘Most mers are born with legs and at the age of three they undergo a ritual celebration where they grow their tails. When they come out of the water, the tail parts and they have legs once again. But the meremers can’t change back. Saegar had a tail when he left Pacifica but if he lost it, then he is a man who will never again be a mer.’’

So much information about a land, a people, a life so alien, Phoebe thought. And yet, it was her land, her people and the roots of her life, she reminded herself.

‘‘Thalassa was the eldest and was sent away in the guardianship of Cyria, your former nanny. And then there is Kai, your twin sister.’’

‘‘My twin?’’ Shock riveted through Phoebe. She had a twin, a sister who had not only shared the first two years of her life, but had also shared their mother’s womb with her.

Tears burned at her eyes as she thought of the sisters and brother and all the time they had lost. The tears burned hotter as she thought of her parents. ‘‘And my mother and father are gone,’’ she said softly.

Kevin’s hand found hers and squeezed it in comfort. She smiled at him, despite the pain that filled her heart for the parents she would never know.

‘‘When your father sent you away, he never dreamed the war would last so long,’’ Loucan said.

"It was his plan to keep you safe away from Pacifica for perhaps as long as a year or so, then reunite with you. He loved you very much."

The words filled Phoebe with a peace and she released her hold on Kevin's hand to swipe away the errant tears that escaped from her eyes.

"Phoebe, Pacifica needs you. Not only could we use your skills as a surgeon, but the people need to know that King Okeana's legacy continues with his children." Loucan leaned forward, his intense gaze pinning her in place. "Return to your home beneath the sea."

Phoebe reached for Kevin's hand once again. "I could never go unless Kevin could go with me."

Loucan nodded. "I assumed as much." He turned his gaze to Kevin. "We need brave men in Pacifica and I would also like you to continue the search for the others. There is no reason why your lives can't be divided between the land and the sea."

Phoebe looked at Kevin, wondering what he thought about the proposition of traveling to Pacifica. "Phoebe, I'll go wherever you want me to go, and there's nothing I would like to do more than find your brother and sisters." He looked at Loucan once again. "I'm still reeling a bit from all this, but we'll go to this Pacifica, just not for a couple of days. There's one important thing we have to do before we go."

"And what's that?" Loucan asked.

Kevin took Phoebe's hand in his. "When we go to

Pacifica, we'll go as husband and wife and that means we have a little thing like a wedding to attend to."

Phoebe's heart exploded with happiness as she realized that eventually she would have the family she'd longed for and in the meantime she had Kevin's love to fill her life.

Loucan stood, as always his features inscrutable and his eyes dark and mysterious. "I will await your call when you are ready to go to Pacifica."

"Loucan?" Phoebe stopped the man before he could leave the room. "What made my tail grow?"

"The tail grows when you are submerged and reach a certain level of salinity. Normally it is a slow and rather painful process. I would guess that your metamorphosis happened quickly due to stress and a high level of adrenaline." He offered her a tight smile. "There are many things yet to explain and to learn before you fully understand the extent of your legacy." He turned and left the room.

Phoebe turned back to Kevin. "A twin," she said softly. "No wonder when you first mentioned Kai's name I felt such a strange feeling of longing."

Kevin stood and pulled her into his arms. "And I will do everything in my power to find them all for you." He smiled at her. "I have a much greater incentive now than just the treasure Loucan might give me. I'll be working for the love and gratitude of my lovely wife."

She returned his smile and wound her arms around his neck. ''You already have that.''

His smile faded and he looked into her eyes for a long moment. ''Five years ago I believed my life ended, that I would never again be happy. Now I'm marrying a beautiful, loving mermaid.''

''Kevin, when you told me about the fear that haunted you that night, twice you told me your greatest fear was that somehow you'd put another officer at risk. That isn't the fear of a coward. That's the fear of a hero.''

His eyes flared with emotion. ''I love you, Phoebe.''

''And I love you,'' she replied, her heart overflowing as his lips claimed hers in a kiss.

''Just one more thing,'' he murmured as he moved his mouth from her lips to her neck.

''What's that?'' she asked, sweet sensations of passion sweeping through her.

''Do you think it's possible our kids will be minnows?''

She jerked her head back to look at him, relaxing as she saw the teasing glint in his eyes. ''You're bad,'' she said and slapped him lightly on his chest.

He laughed and pulled her more intimately against him. ''And the minute we get married I intend to show you just how bad I can be.''

Flames of desire ignited in Phoebe at his words.

"We're going to have our happily-ever-after, Kevin, aren't we?"

"The whole truth and nothing but the truth? Yes, darling, we're going to have our happily-ever-after." Once again his lips claimed hers in a kiss that filled her soul with warmth, with joy...with love.

* * * * *

Don't miss
the next exciting installment
in the Silhouette Romance miniseries,
A TALE OF THE SEA,
with the August 2002 release of
IN DEEP WATER
(RS1608)

A powerful earthquake ravages Southern California...

Thousands are trapped beneath the rubble...

The men and women of Morgan Trayhern's team face their most heroic mission yet...

A brand-new series from
USA TODAY bestselling author

LINDSAY McKENNA

Don't miss these breathtaking stories of the triumph of love!

Look for one title per month from each Silhouette series:

August: THE HEART BENEATH
(Silhouette Special Edition #1486)

September: RIDE THE THUNDER
(Silhouette Desire #1459)

October: THE WILL TO LOVE
(Silhouette Romance #1618)

November: PROTECTING HIS OWN
(Silhouette Intimate Moments #1185)

Available at your favorite retail outlet

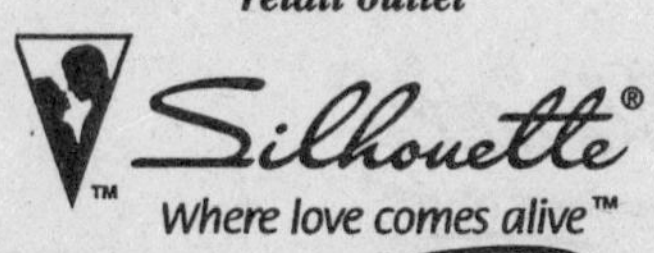

Visit Silhouette at www.eHarlequin.com

SXSMMUR

COMING NEXT MONTH

#1606 THE PRINCESS HAS AMNESIA!—Patricia Thayer
Crown and Glory
Who was the beauty that fell from the sky—right into former FBI agent Jake Sanderstone's mountain refuge? Ana was bossy, stricken with amnesia and…a princess! But when her memory came flooding back, would she let go of love and return to royalty?

#1607 FALLING FOR THE SHEIK—Carol Grace
A bad fall at a ski run left Rahman Harun helpless—and he hated it. But when private nurse Amanda Reston entered his family's cabin, the strong sheik decided he needed her tender, loving care! Her nurturing nature healed his body. Could she also heal his wounded heart?

#1608 IN DEEP WATERS—Melissa McClone
A Tale of the Sea
Kai Waterton had been warned to stay away from the sea.That didn't stop her from heading an expedition to find a sunken ship—or falling for single dad and salvager Ben Mendoza! But what would happen to their budding romance when the mysteries of her past were uncovered…?

#1609 THE LAST VIRGIN IN OAKDALE—Wendy Warren
Be Eleanor's "love tutor"? Cole Sullivan was shocked. His once-shy buddy in high school, now a tenderhearted veterinarian, had chosen her former crush to initiate her in the art of lovemaking. But Cole found himself with second thoughts…and third thoughts…all about Eleanor!

#1610 BOUGHT BY THE BILLIONAIRE—Myrna Mackenzie
The Wedding Auction
When Maggie Todd entered herself in a charity auction, she'd never anticipated being asked to pretend to be royalty! As the wealthy charmer Ethan Bennington tutored the unsophisticated yet enticing Maggie in becoming a "lady," he found he wanted her to become *his* lady….

#1611 FIRST YOU KISS 100 MEN…—Carolyn Greene
Being the Mystery Kisser was easy for columnist Julie Fasano—at first. Anonymously writing about kissing men got more difficult when she met up with investigator Hunter Matthews. Hunter was determined to find the kisser's identity—would he discover her little secret as *they* shared kisses?